THE TRAIL TO
DEVIL'S CANYON

Anton Kozlov has escaped Russia and made a new life for himself on Battle Mountain in Nevada. When he's asked to do a favor for a US Cavalry officer — retrieve a mail-order bride from a stage station — it sounds easy enough ... until he learns that the stage has broken down near a notorious nest of outlaws. Though he succeeds in rescuing Lucy, the way back to Devil's Canyon is fraught with danger — and upon their arrival, there's further trouble in store ...

COLE MATTHEWS

THE TRAIL TO DEVIL'S CANYON

Complete and Unabridged

LINFORD
Leicester

First published in Great Britain in 2018 by
Robert Hale
an imprint of The Crowood Press
Wiltshire

First Linford Edition
published 2021
by arrangement with The Crowood Press
Wiltshire

*A catalogue record for this book is available
from the British Library.*

ISBN 978–1–4448–4676–8

Published by
Ulverscroft Limited
Anstey, Leicestershire

Set by Words & Graphics Ltd.
Anstey, Leicestershire
Printed and bound in Great Britain by
T J Books Ltd., Padstow, Cornwall

This book is printed on acid-free paper

The Mountains — grow unnoticed —
Their Purple figures rise
Without attempt — Exhaustion —
Assistance — or Applause —

In Their Eternal Faces
The Sun — with just delight
Looks long — and last — and golden —
For fellowship — at night —
       Emily Dickinson (1830–1886)

What place is besieged, and vainly
   tries to raise the siege?
Lo, I send to that place a commander,
   swift, brave, immortal,
And with him horse and foot, and
   parks of artillery,
And artillery-men, the deadliest that
   ever fired gun.
       Walt Whitman (1819–1892)

Halfway down the trail to Hell in a
   shady meadow green,
are the Souls of all dead troopers camped
   near a good old-fashion canteen,

and this eternal resting place is known
  as Fiddlers' Green.

Marching past, straight through to
  Hell, the Infantry are seen,
accompanied by the Engineers, Artillery and Marine,
for none but the shades of Cavalrymen dismount at Fiddlers' Green.

Though some go curving down the
  trail to seek a warmer scene,
no trooper ever gets to Hell ere he's
  emptied his canteen
and so rides back to drink again with
  friends at Fiddlers' Green.

And so when man and horse go down
  beneath a saber keen,
or in a roaring charge of fierce melee
  you stop a bullet clean,
and the hostiles come to get your scalp,
  just empty your canteen
and put your pistol to your head and
  go to Fiddlers' Green.
Anon, nineteenth-century Irish poem

Author's Note

The Plains Cavalry

The United States Cavalry existed in countless forms from 1775 to 1942. The cavalry this book is about to describe is the one that existed from 1865 to 1890 and was informally known as the Plains Cavalry. Formed at the end of the Civil War in 1865, the Plains Cavalry was charged with protecting American settlers, railroaders, wagon trains, businesses, gold seekers and others from Indian attacks. It was meant to operate chiefly on the western frontiers of the expanding nation. At that time, almost anything west of the Mississippi River was considered the frontier. Most Americans living east of the Mississippi had no idea of the danger, deprivation or hardship encountered by those who lived on the other side of the river. The cavalry's orders were to combat the ongoing 'Indian problem'.

After the Civil War, the Plains Cavalry was overrun with commissioned officers. Many had held high brevet or temporary ranks during the late war. These temporary promotions were the rewards given for the performance of meritorious sendee. The officers were not always deserving of their ranks. Ex-Colonels now served as Captains and Captains were now Lieutenants. These men were entitled to wear the insignia of the highest brevet rank they had held in the Civil War. Filling the enlisted ranks was another story. Most of the men who had served during the war were finished with fighting and returned to their families. Non-commissioned officers who had served as officers in the Confederate Army filled part of the void. A number of years passed before ex-confederate officers were allowed to serve in the cavalry as commissioned officers. Some of the more adventurous men with Civil War service, also filled the non-commissioned ranks of the new regiments. It was extremely difficult to recruit men for this problematic, hazardous and sometimes fatal duty.

In some ways, the Plains Cavalry was America's version of the French Foreign Legion. Like the Foreign Legion, the cavalry became a place to simply disappear. Most cavalry units operated outside the borders of the states and provided a new start in life with few questions asked. Early on, many of those enlisting in the cavalry had arrest warrants outstanding for them. Some joined the service as an alternative to serving jail time. Some judges believed that a hitch in the military would make a man out of the boy. The ranks of the enlisted were filled with criminals, adventurers and many ex-confederate officers now serving as corporals and sergeants.

Several forts, both large and small, were set up, from the cold northern Dakota, Nebraska, Utah and Montana Territories to the hot desert areas of Texas, New Mexico and Arizona. As the western borders of the United States expanded, so did the areas covered by the cavalry. In some ways, garrison life in a fort was considered a picnic compared to being on patrol or being on a campaign. It was also totally mundane, boring and unrewarding. Experienced soldiers preferred being in the field.

1

Showdown in Devil's Canyon

It was the hour before nightfall.

Reaching for his muzzle-loading Hawken rifle, Anton Kozlov downed the last of his coffee and walked out of his cabin. He slid the percussion 'plains' rifle into its saddle scabbard and swung effortlessly into the saddle. Tall and lean in the fading light, he gathered his sorrel's reins, told his mongrel dog to sit guard and then rode Socks away from the three-roomed log cabin he had raised with his own bare hands, in the fall less than two years before.

Kozlov, or as he was more familiarly known by many of the locals as 'Old Moscow', had been born in Russia, near the River Moskwa, in the vicinity of the City of Moscow. At the age of sixteen he was conscripted and forced into the Russian Army near the end of the war with

7

Napoléon. He witnessed the conflagration of Moscow, and followed the eagles of the French in their disastrous retreat towards the Nieman. It was a favorite theme for the old man to describe the scenes he underwent during that terrible campaign; how, morning after morning, the French soldiers would be found dead about the bivouac fire, lying in the position in which the sleep of death overtook them during the night.

A cross of the Legion of Honour, taken from the dead body of a French officer at the crossing of the River Beresina, the old man was in the habit of exhibiting, and while looking at it would explain: 'How I did pity the poor French!' He used to say Winter came on early that year—in October —as a punishment to Bonaparte. Leaving the army after the capture of the French Emperor, Anton came to Quebec, and afterwards, was for many years in the service of the Hudson Bay Company.

Some twelve years ago, he came to the Bighorn Mountains, where he used to fit out each Winter for trapping expeditions on the head waters of the Wind and Bighorn Rivers here in Devil's Canyon. It was a singular sight to see the old man as he was on the point of starting out in the Fall to his Winter quarters. His uncouth-looking little mule, which he had laden with traps, kettles, cooking utensils and other camping apparatus, until scarcely any mule but ears were visible, had died a month earlier.

Recently, an exploring party in that vicinity were attracted to the hut by the mournful howling of his mongrel dog. Guided by the sound, their steps were directed to the cabin, where a strange, sad sight met their gaze. Near the entrance lay the body of the diminutive mule, dead a few weeks. Beside it sat the dog, who on the approach of the men, ran into the cabin as though to apprise his master that help was near. The ground had been too frozen to bury the creature. With the help of these explorers, Anton was able to inter the mule and they went on their way, leaving him be.

Kozlov guided the sorrel across the shallow, icy creek and took the deer track.

It was a trail he knew well, having traveled it many times to set and check his traps.

He had waged a ceaseless war against beaver and moose and other types of nature's harmless creatures, against wolf and wolverine, and other types of nature's destructive agents; against traders who were rivals and Indians who were hostiles, a trapper like Anton almost, seemed a type of nature's arch-destroyer.

The country was as pretty as a dream. The world seemed to be made up completely of prairie, mountain and forest. It was a world where the trapper moved with a skill and silence as any creature that inhabited that world. With the tools of the trade—cruel steel traps, and the true aim of his rifle—a trapper existed to live off the animals and land. The life was a harsh one, full of misery, weather, and endless hours of work. The reality of the life of a trapper was not immune from being hunted. And most of the times, they were hunted more than the creatures were. They were hunted by both beasts and men alike.

Crusted whiteness clung to the banks. It was here that the frontiersman had set his traps. Kozlov dismounted and secured Socks to a sweeping, low-slung branch of a spruce tree.

He pulled the Hawken rifle from its scabbard and rolled a smoke with his free hand. His keen eyes roamed over the canyon, taking in the traps he had set on the previous morning. One held a gray fox. He would use the fine winter pelt or sell it to the trader. There was nothing in the other fur traps, but his supper was waiting in the squirrel trap.

Anton Kozlov leaned against a pine tree and waited. The day was cloudy, cold and windy.

For the last two days, something had been robbing the trap line. He had found traces of fur and blood on iron jaws, and now he was ready for the predator.

He finished his cigarette. Dressed in buckskins, Kozlov fused with the deepening dusk. In a country of tall men, he stood head and shoulders above most. He'd once had raven-black hair, now turned gray or 'silver' as he liked to call it, which spilled shabbily from beneath his fur hat, and framed a craggy, leathery face. It was a face hardened by sixty-four years with many under the frontier sun and bitter mountain winds. He had deep brown eyes, keen and piercing still. His nose was bulbous, and his firm jaw warned that this was not a man to take lightly despite his advanced years. Few would call Anton Kozlov good-looking, but when he paid an occasional visit to the distant town of Manderson Wells, women turned their heads to watch him pass. It could have also been his stench.

The soft beat of wings betrayed a bird returning to its shelter as the sun began to dip below the dark western rims.

Then Kozlov heard the loud, abrupt crack of a frozen twig. Reaching for his Hawken rifle, he let his eyes sweep the canyon. Swiftly he caught sight of movement. The branches of a spruce shook and dropped a tiny shower of snow. A lone rider guided his pony down into the canyon. Like Kozlov, he was clad in buckskins. He was thin and sinewy. His face was ancient, and his scant hair was white as the snow on his shoulders.

Kozlov recognized the old man as a Northern Paiute. He looked down his rifle sights as the rider approached the squirrel trap. The frontiersman looked around at the darkening trees. He saw no other movement—this Paiute was alone.

He watched the Indian get off his shaggy pony.

The horse moseyed a few paces as the old warrior bent over the dead squirrel.

Anton let the white-haired Indian pry the iron jaws apart. Then he padded to the rim of the canyon.

'Don't you move,' Kozlov said, in the Paiute language, and his grasp of it cut the silence like a steel knife. 'There is a gun pointed at your head.'

The old Paiute Indian froze. Squatted by the trap, he held the limp squirrel aloft and stared at the white man.

'I'm a-comin' down,' Kozlov said, his Russian accent nearly gone with his years in North America. 'You just hold still.'

The old Indian's eyes were faced straight-ahead as he waited.

'Since when do the Paiute steal food?' Anton asked.

Anger darkened the Indian's face and he replied, 'My people are not thieves!'

'You are a thief!' Anton accused, looking down his rifle sights.

'I am old,' the Indian told him. 'I can no longer hunt with the younger men.'

'Heck, neither can I as I am old too,' said Kozlov. He paused and then asked, 'What are you called?'

'Looks At The Bear,' the old Paiute Indian replied gently.

'Now you listen to me, Looks At The Bear,' Kozlov said. 'I once wintered with the Northern Paiute. I learned your ways and your tongue. I know that when a warrior grows old, the younger men hunt for him.'

'Looks At The Bear has pride,' the old Indian simply said.

'So, you have been robbin' my traps and takin' back meat, pretendin' you are still a hunter,' Kozlov said. 'You lie to yourself and to your tribe.'

'Does this small squirrel mean so much that you will shoot me with your fire stick?' Looks At The Bear challenged.

There was silence between the two older men, and for the first time, the Indian's face betrayed a twitch of fear.

'Put my meat down,' ordered Kozlov.

Reluctantly, the Northern Paiute lowered the dead squirrel.

'Your hand is close to your knife,' Kozlov said softly. 'I wouldn't try it if I were you. This rifle would blow your head off before you could throw that knife.'

The old Indian stared at Anton. 'Looks At The Bear is not a fool.'

'Then keep your hand real clear of that knife and stand up,' Kozlov advised.

The Northern Paiute rose to his feet slowly. He appeared frail and vulnerable in the last light of the day. The whispering, rising wind stirred the thin, white hair.

'Listen to me, Looks At The Bear,' Anton said. 'I am not goin' to spill blood. You will ride back to your village alive. But if I catch you robbin' my traps again, I may forget you are an old man.' He motioned with his rifle. 'And take a piece of advice. Tell the young men that your eyes are dim, and you can no longer hunt.'

'I will tell them,' the old Indian said resignedly.

'Now ride home, Looks At The Bear,' Kozlov directed.

The Paiute Indian started to shuffle towards his shaggy pony. He took a last, rueful look at the dead squirrel and climbed on to his pony's bony back.

'Hell, Old Moscow, you are not gonna let this thieving old Indian just ride out!'

The loud taunt came from a rider dressed in a blue cavalry uniform.

Dark, curly hair spilled over his high forehead. His face was in shadow and his eyes, sighting down the barrel of an army rifle, were fixed on the old Indian.

'Stay out of my business, Judd,' Anton told him frankly.

'Now that's no way to welcome your own kin.' The newcomer grinned. 'I came to pay you a visit, and as it turns out, I arrived just in time. Like I said, I covered you — just in case this thieving devil tried anything.' Judd Reed leaned forward in his saddle and snickered. 'You are kinda slipping, Old Moscow! You didn't hear or see us coming … '

The man wasn't really kin. Anton had married his mother — Beulah Reed — years ago, before disease took her shortly after. The boy's father had left long before he had arrived.

'I heard you and I saw you,' Kozlov said coldly. 'You can tell Troopers Yacey, Gravens, and Copeland and the beanpole I don't know, to come out of that thicket now. We are not facin' a war party, just an old man lookin' for food.'

'The beanpole's name is Trooper Alan Loomis — he was posted to Fort Bighorn a few weeks ago,' Judd said coolly. 'If you saw us coming, why didn't you let us know?'

'Why are you here? I didn't ask you to come,' Anton said bluntly.

Lieutenant Reed spat into the snow and then said, 'You are a damn ungrateful cuss, my step-father … huh?'

'Looks At The Bear, I told you to go,' Anton Kozlov reminded the old Indian in the Paiute tongue.

'The redskin goes nowhere!' Anton's former stepson snapped, keeping his Hawken rifle trained on the old Indian warrior. 'He was caught stealing white man's property, and he needs to be taught a lesson.' He jerked his chin, and four uniformed riders emerged from the thicket. 'I would say a permanent one … '

The troopers rode closer. Lean, sly-faced Tuck Gravens came first. Behind him rode Trooper Ben Copeland, a scar-faced professional with receding yellow hair and cold eyes. Hal Yacey was just as Anton Kozlov remembered him from Fort Bighorn — fat and balding with a pencil-thin mustache which looked like a third lip had been drawn. The fourth rider, Loomis, drifted in last.

Anton walked deliberately to stand beside the Indian's shaggy pony. The Northern Paiute remained motionless, his old eyes reading death in the circle of troopers.

'I will say this just once, dear stepson,' Anton Kozlov told the cavalryman. 'It is my trap the Indian stole from and I have decided to let him go. You're not wearing a tin star, so this is none of your damn business.' He lifted the rifle. 'Looks At The Bear is going now, and I will kill the first blue-belly soldier who fires on him.'

Anton slapped the pony's rump, and the old man started to ride slowly across the canyon. The four troopers on the rim sat saddle, bewildered, their rifles aimed at the Northern Paiute Indian as they awaited the lieutenant's order. Anton just looked straight at his soldier 'kin'. He saw Judd's eyes narrow to twin slits. He heard the crunch of hoofs in snow as the Indian moved away. Judd's lips curled into a twisted, frosty smile.

'You always was an Injun-lover, Old Moscow,' the cavalryman sneered softly. 'That is why you quit the army back in Russia.'

'Is this a social call, Judd?' Anton demanded.

'Not exactly,' Judd Reed muttered. 'I am here to hire your services.'

Kozlov watched old Looks At The Bear ride past Trooper Hal Yacey and vanish safely into the dusk.

'You are wastin' your time,' Anton said flatly in response. 'I am not interested in bein' an army scout again. I reckon you will remember the stories I told you and your mother.'

There was a moment's silence between the two men.

'I am not here on Major Peabody's account,' Judd told him. 'I want to hire you for myself, for something personal.'

The old man eyed his once stepson intently. 'Go on, you have my attention.'

'Anton, you're not being exactly hospitable,' Judd complained. 'We rode all day to get here. I reckon the least you could do is to offer us grub and coffee.'

Anton walked to the second trap and retrieved the dead fox. Keeping the five uniformed riders waiting, he set the traps again.

'C'mon, follow me back to the cabin,' he said finally as he returned to his horse.

He should have been pleased to see Judd — it was the first time in almost two years. It helped remind him of Beulah. Instead, Anton considered the soldiers as intruders. Maybe their very uniforms reminded him of a part of his life he wanted to forget. There was a full moon rising as Anton headed into the canyon he had made his home. He saw the lights of the settlers' cabins. The timber-wolves which ranged along the stark ridges, bayed in the distance. He forded the creek, and his mongrel dog barked a greeting. Kozlov spoke quietly to the ugly-faced dog he had inherited when mountain man Cassius Stoddard died from a snake bite about nine months earlier. Anton dismounted and then motioned the blue-coats to tether their horses and come inside.

Cassius Stoddard had enlisted as a private with 'The Lewis and Clark Expedition' in the autumn of 1803 at Maysville, Kentucky. He was stipulated five dollars a month pay after answering the ad for 'good hunters, stout, healthy, unmarried men, accustomed to the woods and capable of bearing bodily fatigue in a pretty considerable degree'. Cassius had told Anton of the hardships and triumphs of the expedition, as well as routine adventures in hunting, starving, Indian diplomacy, and getting chased by grizzly bears. In August of 1806 the expedition reached the Mandan villages. It was there that Cassius was granted permission by the explorers to take his leave and he next joined two trappers from Illinois, Forrest Hancock and Joseph Dickson, bound for the Yellowstone River.

It was told that Cassius Stoddard alone paddled canoe down the Missouri to the mouth of the Platte where he found keelboats of the Missouri Fur Company of St. Louis, led by Manuel Lisa. He was promptly recruited and went with this expedition up the Missouri and the Yellowstone to the mouth of the Bighorn River, where he eventually made his home. This is where he had first met Anton Kozlov, teaching him the tricks of the trade of being a frontier mountain man.

Anton had built a cabin of three rooms. Its main room was a parlor with a potbelly stove right in the middle, its chimney through the roof. A door in the western wall opened into his bedroom. The third room was used for pelt storage.

'Make yourself at home,' he said, as he lit a flint-glass, kerosene lamp.

Lieutenant Judd Reed straddled a chair. He was not even thirty, and already was sporting a few gray hairs. They sprouted from his temples. Once lean and rangy, the lieutenant, now had a roll of fat hanging over his belt. Trooper Yacey stood behind the lieutenant, probably aware that Anton Kozlov had never liked him. Gravens and Copeland found chairs and waited for the coffee to heat. The youngest soldier, Alan Loomis, was still in his teens. His clean-shaven face was boyish and his eyes relatively innocent. Maybe he had been spared what Anton had once seen, so far at least.

'Get straight to the point, Judd,' Anton said, as the cavalrymen drank their coffee and ate his cold biscuits.

The lieutenant lit a cigar and then said, 'Anton, I want you to ride west to Bear Creek Pass and collect a woman.'

'I reckon you need to explain that a bit further,' Anton said.

'It ain't complicated,' Judd said. 'A woman named Miss Lucy Doniphon is coming to Bear Creek Pass on the Cheyenne & Black Hills Stage Line. She arrives exactly a week from today. She is expecting me to meet her at the stage depot, but due to circumstances, I can't do that ... '

'Major Peabody sent us out on patrol,' Trooper Hal Yacey mumbled into his coffee mug.

24

'My orders are to track down and bring back three army deserters,' Judd hastily supplied.

'You will enjoy that,' Anton remarked wryly.

'I would rather be meeting Miss Doniphon,' Judd snapped irritably.

'What is this Lucy Doniphon to you?' Kozlov asked.

Judd Reed blew smoke into the air before he said, 'She is to be my bride.'

The cavalryman's pronouncement hung like the cigar smoke between them.

'I reckon congratulations is in order, Judd,' Anton said mildly.

'I will invite you to the wedding,' the soldier stated flatly.

The man known as Old Moscow to most, glanced back at the blue-clad trooper. 'Where did you meet her?'

'Well, I haven't met her, as of yet,' Judd told him reluctantly. 'She is what is known as a mail-order bride.'

'Mail-order?'

'White women are in short supply out west,' the lieutenant said stiffly. 'I

25

reckon you know that, Old Moscow.' He snickered. 'For instance, I don't see a bed-warmer in your place! Time to move on from my mother.' He exhaled more smoke. 'Some men might settle for Injun squaws, but that is not good enough for an officer in the United States Army. I paid money to McQuarry's Matrimonial News in San Francisco. They specifically run personal ads. for men and women seeking marriage. They helped me find my bride.'

'A woman you have never seen before?' Anton said, shaking his head in disbelief.

'McQuarry's sent me a portrait of her,' Judd said defensively. 'She happens to be quite beautiful.'

'And has she seen your picture, Judd?' Anton asked, with a hint of a smile.

'Um ... no,' the lieutenant said, flicking ash from his cigar tip. 'There are no cameras in Fort Bighorn.'

Old Moscow leaned back in his chair and sipped his coffee. 'Uh-huh ... It is a long trail to Bear Creek Pass,' Anton added without further comment.

'I don't expect you to do this out of the kindness of your Russian heart,' Judd assured him. 'I am gonna pay you. I am offering you one hundred dollars to fetch my bride and escort her back here. You can hand her over to me in exactly two weeks' time, right here at this here cabin. By then, we will have those damn deserters and she can ride to the fort with all of us.'

Anton Kozlov downed his coffee. He didn't like being away from his cabin for too long of time, but a hundred dollars was a lot of money, and he could certainly use it. The fur trade was declining. Shorter and less dangerous overland routes were established from the trapping areas to the larger markets, thus driving down their worth. The whims of fashion were also beginning to dictate that silk hats replace beaver hats. Anton had also heard of a new process being created to make good felt, cheaper than using fur. And to top all of that, beaver was getting mighty scarce. He'd had no regular employment or pay since he had quit scouting for Fort Bighorn. Not that he had ever felt any regrets. It had been his choice. He glanced at the lieutenant. Judd was still blowing smoke and looking around the little cabin with disdain. Anton didn't particularly want to work for this cavalry officer, but one hundred dollars would be a big help.

'I will fetch your mail-order bride for you,' Kozlov decided.

'I will pay you fifty dollars now and fifty on Miss Doniphon's safe delivery,' Judd said in a very businesslike manner.

'Um … sure … suits me just fine,' Anton mumbled.

'She arrives on the noon stage one week from today,' Judd informed him as he pulled an envelope from his pocket. 'You will need to know what she looks like.' He opened the envelope and pulled out a faded photograph which he handed to the old fur trapper. 'This is my woman, soon to be bride.'

The pallid lantern light played over the glazed surface of the portrait. Lucy Doniphon's face was young, and a spark of defiance showed in her wide eyes. She had full lips and long, unruly hair which apparently had not been combed, not even for the studio photographer.

'You have done well for yourself, Judd,' Anton complimented him.

Judd flicked more ash from the tip of his cigar as he said, 'You should get yourself a woman too, Old Moscow It is not good for a man to live alone. Leastways, that is what the preacher who is gonna marry us quoted to me.'

'I will have her here in two weeks from today,' Kozlov said, accepting the officer's down payment of fifty dollars.

The men had nothing more to say, and Judd stood up to go.

'Let's go find those lousy deserters,' Judd said to his men.

'Hell's bells, it is night already!' Trooper Tuck Gravens whined.

'There is bright moonlight,' Judd snapped, as his eyes ranged over the four cavalrymen. 'I want you all in the saddle_on the double!'

As the troopers leapt to obey, Judd

smirked in satisfaction. He enjoyed giving orders. The army was a perfect career choice for him.

'Old Moscow … um … Anton … '

The old man eyed the cavalry officer. 'Yes?'

'Keep the portrait,' the lieutenant said. 'You might need to identify her.'

'Sure...as you wish.'

'One more thing,' Judd Reed said, his eyes narrowing. 'She is mine. Keep your dirty, old paws off her.'

'So long, Judd,' Anton replied softly.

When the cavalry riders were gone, Anton Kozlov made fresh coffee and looked again at Lucy Doniphon's portrait. There was more than a hint of defiance in those fiery eyes. There was resentment, even anger.

2

Old Moscow Meets Lucy Doniphon

The trip to Bear Creek Pass had been fairly eventful for Anton Kozlov. He arrived at Lewis' fork along the Snake River, one of the largest rivers in the area. It took him all day to cross. It is half a mile wide, deep and rapid. The way he managed was this: he unloaded his mule — which he had bought to replace the one he lost, and to use to haul Lucy back — and swam across with his horse — Socks. In returning, the new mule, by treading on a round stone, stumbled and threw him off, and the current was so strong that a bush which he was able to catch hold of, saved him from drowning.

Then finally, a week later and a couple hours before noon, Anton came out of the bluegrass prairie, forded Grapevine Creek and headed his sorrel stallion into Bad Pass. The pass had earned its name from other mountain men and was part of a much larger web of commerce and interaction between the native people and traders. It was a rough and unpleasant route to most unseasoned travelers, but not to men like Anton Kozlov. It wasn't just the terrain that caused problems; many a mountain man had encountered grizzly bear, Crow, Paiute, Shoshone and Blackfoot Indians along the trail.

He was almost at trail's end.

It was a cool, gray day and yesterday's storm clouds still hung in the sky like rumpled curtains. Anton — Old Moscow — rode faster when he reached the wagon trail on the high side of the pass. He passed a cabin and raised his hand to greet the first white man he had seen since leaving Devil's Canyon. The trail circled an unprosperous-looking Indian camp and a clump of spruce trees. Then it passed the signboard announcing:

BEAR CREEK PASS – pop. 141

Approaching the town limits, Kozlov

noticed two men loading a rocking chair into the back of a wagon. The slight wind whispering down the pass, made the hooped canvas tremble. A tall woman with a baby in her arms, watched as the men, one silver-bearded and the other half his age, secured the chair with ropes. Finally, she gathered her skirts with one hand, and climbed on to the wagon seat. The family was almost ready for the long westerly trek as Kozlov drew alongside.

'Good morning, mister,' the silver-bearded man greeted him.

'Howdy,' Anton replied.

After appraising him in a kindly way, the man said, 'Looks as if you have traveled a long way … '

'For sure,' Anton responded. 'From past Devil's Canyon, near the Bighorn Mountains.'

'That is on our map, Seth,' the woman said, rocking the stirring baby gently.

'Hush … I know that, Maude,' the man replied as he looked back at the rider. 'We are headed west of there, to the new settlement of Medicine Flats,' he paused. 'How the trail, mister?'

'No trouble between Devil's Canyon and here,' Anton politely told him.

'No Indian sign or trouble?' the younger man asked impatiently.

'Sure, but no war paint,' Kozlov told him.

'Good! Praise the Lord!' the woman exclaimed.

'But west of Devil's Canyon is Northern Paiute country,' Anton added, 'and that is another story. I would make sure to travel with other wagons there.' He looked at the woman and her baby. 'In fact, I will give you a piece of advice. I wouldn't even go that far without company if I was you. The Indians in these parts aren't on the warpath, but there is always the risk that a few young bucks will be tempted by the sight of a single wagon.'

'I have faith, mister. The good Lord will protect us,' Seth said with confidence.

Anton nodded. 'I sure hope so.'

'We leave in a few minutes,' Seth

smugly proclaimed.

'So long, safe travels,' Kozlov said, riding past the wagon and turning into town.

Bear Creek Pass was a disorderly mass of delicate structures and a few wagons converted into temporary living quarters. It stretched along both sides of the wide, deeply-rutted main street. The big hanging clock outside Le Tourneau's Trading Post showed ten minutes to noon.

There was a new church, the Divine Tabernacle. A group of women tightly wrapped in woolen shawls stood outside, chatting to the young preacher. Old Moscow passed the law office. It was closed. Sometimes Bear Creek Pass had a resident lawman, sometimes not. Last time he had been to the town, Sheriff Tony Stinson had been wearing the badge. From the look of the cobwebbed windows and padlocked front door, the lawman had either left or was resting in a pine box or off chasing some fugitives. The town boasted two saloons, one oddly named Prudence Hotel.

The other, a more flashy and raucous establishment, was called The Babylon House. He glanced down the street. Past the stock corrals and the half-finished schoolhouse stood Ma Boyle's Rooms. Right opposite the rooming house was the austere Cheyenne & Black Hills office and depot. The long planks of the raised platform fronting the office appeared to be deserted — there seemed to be no towners awaiting the incoming noon stagecoach.

Anton Kozlov rode right up to the platform, swung out of the saddle and looped Socks' and the mule's reins over a tie rail. He climbed the platform steps and looked east for the expected cloud of dust. His eyes caught no movement. He was about to build a cigarette when the office door slapped open. The Cheyenne & Black Hills Stage Line clerk looked him over and grimaced.

'You here for the noon stage, mister?' the clerk guessed.

Anton nodded. 'That's right.'

'Didn't you read the plain notice I

36

pinned on the Prudence wall?' the man snapped.

'I didn't stop for a drink. I haven't been to the Prudence,' Kozlov said. 'I rode straight here.'

'No doubt to meet a passenger?' the clerk guessed again.

Anton nodded again. 'That's right, her name is Lucy Doniphon.'

'Well, mister, I hope you have time on your hands. Wire came early this morning.' He sniffed as he explained. 'Bear Creek Pass is almost civilized now; Western Union's arrived.'

'And what is your point?' Kozlov demanded.

'OK, OK, mister,' the clerk said, shuffling his papers. 'The wire came from Lacey's Station. There has been trouble along the trail. Seems the westbound threw an axle and hit a boulder. It is a wreck. Horses snapped out of harness and stampeded off, leaving everyone stranded. The driver has a broken leg, and the passengers are shook up but no worse for the wear. The guard walked back to Lacey's to send the wire, but the passengers and the driver went to Sylvester Earhart's to wait for the next stage, a week from now.'

'Earhart's Post is a hell hole,' Anton said taciturnly. 'It is no place for a woman.'

The Cheyenne & Black Hills Stage Line clerk spread his hands.

'If you don't like your woman being there, I guess you had better ride out and collect her.'

'She is not *my* woman,' the old trapper clarified.

The clerk raised his bushy eyebrows and said, 'Do what you like, mister. Leave her there, ride out and fetch her. It is your choice. But if she doesn't catch the next stage, I am not allowing a refund for the miles between Earhart's and here.'

Anton 'Old Moscow' Kozlov remounted his sorrel horse as the clerk returned to his dime novel and tepid coffee.

The sun burst through the gray cloud cover as he followed the stage trail down the pass. An eagle soared majestically overhead as the rider passed an old cabin raised by a mountain man, ten years before covered wagons entered the pass. Though roughly constructed, there was an air of nicety and comfort about it, which could hardly be expected in a frontier log-house. On the outside, the walls presented a comparatively smooth surface, though a glance would be sufficient to satisfy one that the work was of the axe and not of the plane. Anton had been here before. On the inside, the walls seemed to be plastered with a material which, in its primitive state, resembled stiff, brown clay; and it was through a chimney of the same substance that the smoke of the fire within found vent.

An Indian squaw stood in the shadow of the rude doorway. Her hair, as dark as the memory of childhood days, floated in soft ringlets over her exquisitely-formed shoulders, half concealing in its wavy flow her lovely cheeks, mantling with the rich hue of a rough life — cheeks which, long ago, might have been tinged with the sun's brown dye, but which now, miracle though it might seem, bore little trace of the sun's scorching hand, or tell-tale mark of western life on the plains or in the mountains. She had blue eyes, and a lovely light lingered in their liquid depths, while her form was one corresponding to her face: slender, but lithe and springing. She appeared well calculated to endure, along with a stout heart; the hardships that must come upon her seemed so strangely out of place.

The old man was still there, motionless on a chair with his spotted dog at his feet. The squaw, half turning, threw up one beautiful arm, and with her hand, shaded her eyes from the glare of the sun, at the same time glancing to the right. As she did, she gave a slight start, for in the distance, she had caught sight of Anton Kozlov. Any cause for fear was, however, quickly removed as she almost immediately recognized him as a friend, murmuring lightly to herself. She looked young enough to be the mountain man's granddaughter, and took a seat beside the dog.

Anton offered a friendly wave and continued on his way. He did not have time to visit.

When he cleared the pass, Anton nudged Socks into a long, steady lope. After a while, he left the stage trail and short-cut across the wide meadow. There he rested the sorrel, drank water from his canteen and smoked two cigarettes. He expected to reach Earhart's by sundown. The delay would probably mean that he would arrive late at Devil's Canyon with the woman ... and Judd would be furious. Well, his former stepson would just have to wait. By the look of that photograph, Miss Lucy Doniphon was worth waiting for.

He turned to the trail and followed it around a ragged saw tooth. It was mid-afternoon, and the shadows began to lengthen. He saw no one on the trail. Despite the growing population in Bear Creek Pass and the push west, this was still a frontier.

The ridge up which Anton Kozlov

labored atop his sorrel horse was a sparsely-timbered slope which terminated in a rounded crest a mile away. To the mule behind him, that smoothly-rolling sky line must have looked like ten miles ahead of it. No breath of wind stirred the stinging, dead air. The slope, which in reality was a very easy grade, assumed the steepness of a mountain side. Anton wanted above all things to sleep. He glanced backward.

A half hour later Anton and his two mounts stood side by side upon the crest of the ridge and looked down into the valley. Both he and the animals were breathing heavily. As they stood now with the sun dancing above them, the cold seemed to press upon them like a thing of weight. The temperature was dropping. The going was easier, but the 'strong cold' seemed to strike to the very bone. After what seemed hours, he found himself at a tributary of the Yellowstone River — the Old Sandy River.

He forded the Old Sandy River at the stage crossing and kept to the trail as it dropped into Colter's Canyon. The setting sun still colored the western rimrock, but it was dark lower down and Kozlov glimpsed the distant lights of Earhart's. Only now the smoke did not rise from the chimney but poured from its mouth and fell heavily to the roof where it rolled slowly to the ground. He slowed Socks to a walk as the shadows closed around him. He heard wild laughter on the wind. Lanterns flickered and swung under the eaves of the barn-like building.

There was another burst of bawdy laughter, and then he heard the dull thud and the clink of bottles. Anton slid from his saddle and tethered Socks to a hitching post. He glanced at the bullet-scarred signboard which informed travelers that redeye, card games, rooms, supplies and ammunition were available. In fact, few bona fide travelers came to Earhart's. The place was a haunt for outlaws, misfits and frontier scum.

He heard raised voices and more mirth as he opened the front door. Smoke shrouded the long, low-roofed room which served as both saloon and store. A fat Indian woman stood behind the bar counter. Rough-faced, bearded men sat hunched over a poker game. Close to the card table were shelves displaying canned food and a stack of flour sacks. Guns rested across wall hooks. At the far end of the room, a stove glowed with heat.

A younger man — a boy compared to the others — was lying on a bench and a woman was seated beside him holding a spoon to his lips while she supported his head on her arm. The 'boy' swallowed and a spoonful of hot liquid trickled down his throat. He appeared to be warming up, and comfortable, and drowsy — so drowsy that it was with an effort that he managed to swallow another spoonful of the hot liquid. Slowly he opened his eye and then struggled to a sitting posture. He became conscious of a stinging sensation in his face and he prodded his cheek with an inquisitive finger.

The woman noticed the action. 'It's not bad,' she explained. 'Your nose and your cheeks were frozen, but I thawed them out with the snow.' Suddenly his expression changed, and a look of fear haunted his eyes.

'Get off me … what is this you're shoveling down my throat?'

Anton moved his gaze to Sylvester Earhart, who was flanked by two smirking men and towered over a young woman whose chair was wedged against the wall. No one noticed Anton 'Old Moscow' Kozlov as he stood in the misty haze.

Earhart had his hands planted on his huge hips as he said, ' … reckon it's time for you to face some cold, hard facts, ma'am … '

'I have been telling you all day — if you would just listen — I am Lieutenant Judd Reed's bride-to-be!' she insisted as the men just snickered. 'He will be waiting for me at the depot. Even though I will be a day late, he will still be there … I know he will … he said … '

'Haw! Haw!' Earhart snickered as he moved closer. 'What did you say your name was again, miss?'

'Lucy Doniphon … '

Kozlov did not need to hear her name. Even though the lantern light was dim and the smoke thick, he recognized her face from her portrait. He could see the same defiant anger in her eyes, but now it was anger laced with fear. Sylvester Earhart and his galoots were gathered like vultures around a banquet.

The vultures slapped their sides in gaiety.

'Sounds like a saloon name to me,' Earhart chortled.

'I have never even been inside a saloon! How dare you?' she flashed.

Kozlov started towards her. The poker players, engrossed in their game, paid him no heed. The squaw made a half-hearted effort to offer him a drink, but he shook her off before she could complete her attempt.

'Ma'am, you ain't exactly a good liar,' Earhart accused. 'First, this Lieutenant Reed of yours, if there is such a feller at all, is an officer. That means he is a gentleman!' He chuckled. 'He certainly wouldn't be marrying a saloon whore. He would choose a real lady, another officer's daughter ... '

'Why ... I ... never ... Leave me alone — please!' she said with disgust.

'Quit playing games now, woman,' Earhart snapped. 'You are alone, and you need a roof over your head. Like I said before, you can work for me.'

She snorted. 'I gave you my answer.'

Sylvester Earhart's eyes narrowed.

'Sure you did, Miss Lucy. Well, ma'am, I will collect what you owe me now.'

She looked at the large man with complete shock. 'What ... what do you mean?'

Anton Kozlov halted a few paces away from the stove.

'Let's see ... you owe me for the bath, two meals, coffee and the use of that table and chair. That adds up to ... roughly nine dollars ... I reckon,' Earhart said.

She stared incredulously at the bearded hulk of a man.

'But–but, Mr Earhart, you told me it

was all on the house,' the woman whispered.

'I don't recall ever saying that.' Earhart grinned. 'Did I say that, Dutton?' the man asked a man at his right elbow.

Dutton Tully leered a broken-tooth smile and shook his head.

'Did you hear me offer this lady free hospitality, Nim?' Earhart asked the other vulture.

'Certainly not, Mr Earhart,' Nim Larkin assured him.

'Nine dollars, Miss Lucy,' Earhart demanded coldly.

'I … I don't have that kind of money,' she said nervously. She looked pleadingly at a plump little man in a dark suit and derby hat who sat huddled over his traveling case.

'Mr Garth, you are a banker … could you please lend me the money?'

Ray Garth glanced at the immense Earhart.

'I might be a banker, ma'am, but right now I am just a stranded traveler — like you. I am carrying no money.'

48

'Looks like you will have to work off your debt, ma'am,' Earhart said solemnly. 'You can start by entertaining Nim in the back room. That shouldn't present a problem for a saloon strumpet.'

Nim Larkin grinned and stumbled eagerly towards her.

'Lay a hand on her and you are a dead man,' Old Moscow Kozlov warned, lifting his pistol.

Larkin froze as the words hung in the sudden stillness. The card players sat like statues. Then, as Kozlov thumbed back his gun hammer, Larkin slowly turned his head. His ugly face was scarred from cheek to chin, and his eyes were narrowed to slits as he appraised the danger of the situation.

'Just who — who the hell are you?' he stammered.

'He is just an old saddle bum,' Earhart sneered. 'I remember he drifted in over a year ago and perhaps before that. Stayed overnight.' He surveyed the man behind the gun. 'I don't recall your name, old man, but whoever you are, mister, keep your nose out of this.'

'Ma'am,' Anton told the woman, 'just pick up your bag and come with me.'

'Like hell she will!' Earhart exploded. 'Dammit, you can't just march in here like you own the place and grab one of my employees …'

'Hurry up, ma'am,' Anton directed Lucy calmly.

Lucy Doniphon hesitated slightly. She looked at the tall, older stranger with the gun, and then contemplated the three men confronting her. She saw the naked lust, in Nim's eyes. Making a sudden decision, she reached for her luggage and stood up.

'Drop that gun, or I will blow you apart!' The harsh demand boomed from behind the bar. 'Now, mister!'

Kozlov glanced sideways and saw a lean, one-eyed man standing beside the petrified squaw. The single eye looked down the two fat barrels of a shotgun.

'Nice work,' Sylvester Earhart complimented him. He smiled coldly at Kozlov then and said, 'Better do what he tells you, old man.'

Kozlov held his six-gun steady as he replied: 'Sure, you could fire that shotgun, but you will get Earhart, Nim, and the other vulture, too.'

The man behind the bar wavered and looked to Earhart for advice. Kozlov grabbed the split-second, angled his gun and pulled the trigger. The bullet smashed high into the shotgunner's shoulder, and the shotgun discharged its heated hail into the ceiling. Pellets blasted two hanging lanterns into fragments, sending hot oil spraying over the trading post. The wounded man dropped his shotgun and clapped his left hand to the bloody mess that had been the joint of his right shoulder Coldly, Anton Kozlov pointed his smoking pistol straight at Earhart's large head.

'Who's next?' he asked the ashen-faced trader.

'Take the whore and get out of here, old man,' Earhart said. 'She ain't worth much anyway.'

'Outside, ma'am,' Kozlov repeated.

Lucy Doniphon edged around the wooden table. Earhart and his companions watched as she moved past the man with the gun. The man with the shattered shoulder collapsed in pain, and the squaw stayed absolutely frozen in place.

'If I see a man walk outside, it will be his last walk,' Anton said with certainty.

He backed to the door and sidled to where the woman waited with his horse and the mule.

'Hook the handle of your travelin' bag over the saddle horn of the horse, ma'am,' Anton told her. His eyes roved along the front wall of the trading post as she did his bidding. 'Now I am goin' to mount up. You climb up on that mule.'

'A mule ... really?' She started to complain; his look stopped that. 'Mister — thank you,' she whispered as Anton swung into his saddle. 'I — I don't even know your name.'

He reached over and grasped her arm but did not hurt her in doing so.

'I will help you up, ma'am.' Still keeping an eye on the building, Anton hauled her up on to the mule's back. 'The name,' he said, 'is Anton Kozlov. People call me Old Moscow.'

'Why?' she asked.

'Time to explain that is later,' he said as he nudged the horse into motion. 'I am an associate of Lieutenant Reed.' He sheathed his pistol. 'Now, grab the reins tight, ma'am. It may be a mule, but he has an ornery streak in him. It can be a bit of a rough ride. I am aimin' to put a lot of distance between us and this post in a real short time.'

Lucy locked her hands on the reins of the mule — the creature was a cross between a donkey stallion or a jack and a horse mare, and Anton and Socks sprinted into the darkness. The mule's conformation was a combination of traits from both parents. The head, hip and legs usually took after the jack. The mule did not have a pronounced arch of the neck. Its hair was thin on the forelock, with coarse mane hair. The mule tried its best to imitate the donkey's bray, but had a more unique sound that was a combination of the horse's whinny and the grunting of the wind-down of a bray, sounding more like: 'Whinee-aw ah aw.' Then men with rifles barged through the door and started hollering at the fleeing foursome. Two bullets thudded into pine trunks as a few of the men began to fire. Another shot kicked dirt ahead of Socks. Then they were in the clear … at least momentarily.

'Um … Mr Kozlov …. I mean … Old Moscow … '

'Quiet, ma'am.'

Anton sat tight in his saddle as Lucy clung to the reins and packs on the mule. He heard the soft, incessant moan of the winter wind. Anton Kozlov was well acquainted with nearly every inch of the country over which he was determined to travel. That said, it did not mean danger was not an obstacle. He was not afraid of immediate pursuit by the men from Earhart's, as there was little profit in coming after them in this cold weather, at least he hoped. Gradually an opening became evident — a rough, seldom-traveled, and almost impracticable pass — apparently extending through into the Montana territory on the other side.

At first, he had expected pursuit but was relieved to hear none. Still, he waited for a full five minutes before continuing.

'Didn't figure Earhart would just let us go, but it seems that way,' he said finally. 'Maybe that skunk just doesn't give a damn.'

'He's a skunk sure enough,' Lucy echoed, 'but at first I thought he was a real gentleman. He allowed me a bath and said the food was free. It was only after a while that I knew what was on his mind.' Her arms struggled in the cold to hold the reins. 'Thank heaven you came, Mr Koz … Old … '

'Call me Anton.'

'OK, Anton.'

Man and beast being so well acquainted with the route, the rate of progress was scarcely diminished. On either side towered the mountains, the almost perpendicular walls covered with draperies of green at the top, where moonlight fell; but lower down, dark and chill. Eyesight could be of little avail here, without a thorough knowledge of the place and its surroundings.

And still, as Anton clattered on, an answering noise from behind, as it were an echo, showed that perhaps they had a pursuer after all. A fearful smile swept over the old man's face as he listened to the noise.

'Judd asked me to meet you at Bear Creek Pass, ma'am,' Anton explained, hoping to keep her mind off the potential pursuer. 'When I got to the depot and heard what had happened, I rode straight there.'

'I was expecting Judd to meet me,' Lucy said, her arms still enfolding some of the packages on the mule. She then asked anxiously, 'Has something happened to Judd?'

'No, he had army business to tend to,' Anton said simply.

'Oh,' she replied.

'He had orders to obey, ma'am,' he

explained.

'Which came before me, I reckon?' she said.

'He had no choice — that is the way it is with the army, ma'am. He had to chase some deserters.'

She nodded. 'So, he sent you … '

'Hired me, actually,' Anton amended.

'Um … hired?' she asked.

'Judd paid me to meet the stage and escort you to my place in Devil's Canyon. Judd will collect you there,' Anton calmly answered.

Lucy hesitated and then asked, 'And — and is it far to this … Devil's Canyon?'

He could feel the thud of her heartbeat. He understood why Lucy Doniphon was apprehensive. She had traveled hundreds of long, dusty miles through a wilderness to meet Lieutenant Judd Reed, the soldier she was set to marry. Instead, she faced the prospect of days and nights on the trail with another man — a strange mountain man to boot. In all probability, the lieutenant would hardly even have mentioned Anton Kozlov in his letters.

'Don't worry, ma'am,' Anton reassured her, 'we will be there shortly... iffen we don't have any bad weather. You shouldn't have to ride that old mule the entire trip.'

'I wasn't complaining, Mr ... Old Mos ... what should I call you?,' she finally asked hastily.

'As I said before, Anton will be just fine, ma'am,' he said. 'There is a horse trader in Bear Creek Pass and he owes me a favor. We will head out now and pay Reuben Glanton a visit. Perhaps we can get you a proper mount.'

The woman looked surprised. 'At this hour?'

'Like I said,' Anton began and added a wink, 'Reuben owes me a favor.'

'Is it a long way to Bear Creek Pass?' she asked.

'If we start now we will be knockin' on Reuben's door this side of midnight.'

3

Deadly Sundown and a Bloody Trail

Reuben Glanton, clad in a nightshirt and a sheepskin coat, opened his stable door and waved his candle-illuminated and unusually-shaped glass globe lantern at the row of stalled horses.

'She is down the back,' the old horse trader said with a yawn. 'Follow me, Moscow.'

Glanton shuffled across the hay-strewn floor, waddling rather than walking. He was completely bald, and a deep, purple scar ran over his scalp from his forehead to the back of his hairless neck.

The horse trader halted by the last stall and thrust his glass globed lantern at a sleepy-eyed, shaggy-maned mare which looked docile, harmless and — more importantly — ancient.

'She is quite the looker, ain't she?'

'This old nag?' Anton fired back.

'No, I mean your woman,' Glanton corrected.

'Not my woman … Lieutenant Judd Reed's,' Anton clarified.

'A damn fine filly,' Glanton muttered as he removed the stall rails. 'She has the kinda body some men would kill to git their grubby paws on!' He kicked the last rail over the straw. 'Here, Moscow, hold the doggone lantern.' He yawned again. 'A purty face, hair like fire and those eyes … don't get me started on those eyes … '

'Don't get you started? Huh? I'm afraid you won't stop,' Anton replied.

'And you are gonna spend a whole week of days — and nights — with her?' The horse trader was wide-eyed.

'I said she ain't my woman, she is engaged to a cavalry officer,' Kozlov reminded the old man.

'Well, I hope he knows enough to look after her properly,' Glanton muttered.

Anton lifted the lantern as Glanton secured the bridle and bit. The old mare snorted but remained still. Finally, the horse trader reached

60

for a battered saddle.

'Thanks for this, Reuben. Keep the mule for me until I return; wish I could bring her along too, but iffen those fellas from Earhart's come after us, be better to have two horses and no mule.'

'I hear ya and no worries about the mule. The horse's name is Fleabag, and there is certainly no hurry to bring this bag of bones back,' Glanton told him.

'Of course, this nag is called Fleabag,' Anton laughed.

Reuben Glanton walked the mare outside.

Lucy was waiting with Glanton's portly wife, Anna. She had used the few minutes to change into warmer clothes.

'You could stay for the rest of the night and ride out in the morning,' Anna Glanton offered.

'That is very kind of you, Anna. Thanks for the offer, but we have been delayed enough already,' Kozlov said. 'I believe Lieutenant Reed will sure be anxious if his bride does not arrive on time.'

'I can understand that,' Glanton

murmured, his eyebrows raised as he appraised Lucy Doniphon.

Kozlov gathered his reins as Lucy climbed into Fleabag's saddle.

They rode slowly at first, while Kozlov let Lucy get used to the mare's gait. He could see that she was not really at home in the saddle … but more at home than being on a pack mule. Well, she would have plenty of time for that to change.

She rode right alongside him, staying close in the night.

'Hold your reins loose, ma'am,' he advised. He saw the 'uh-oh I am not so sure I want to keep riding this horse while it is doing what it does' look on her face. 'Don't be scared of it. If that horse believes you are scared, it likely will be scared also. This old mare won't bolt with you.'

Dogs barked curiously as the riders circled the Indian village. The riders passed the old prospector's cabin and out of the pass. When they reached the river, Lucy's mare stood stubbornly on dry land until Anton leaned over and jerked the bridle. When the two riders began to ford the river, Lucy clutched her saddle horn grimly.

'Just relax, ma'am. Keep your head up. Your horse will be followin' your focus whether that is over the next jump or somewhere down the trail. If you are lookin' nowhere or down, you are goin' to throw off your balance too far forward, puttin' you at risk for fallin' that way should your horse stop suddenly. You could wind up on Fleabag's neck. Keep your eyes and head up, and remember you should always look first to where you want to steer your horse. If you are lookin' nowhere, your horse should be going nowhere.'

'Oh OK … I am trying, Anton,' she said in a strained voice.

'I hope you weren't expectin' Judd to fetch you in some fancy carriage,' he said.

'I–I didn't know what to expect, to be honest with you,' Lucy confessed.

'I have to warn you, we are goin' to ride some rough country,' Anton told her. 'Just listen to me, follow what I do.'

She grimaced but said firmly, 'I will be all right, Mr Koz … I mean … Anton.'

They made the western bank and headed across the long flats.

It was a lengthy time before Kozlov slowed his sorrel and indicated a hollow protected by a rocky ledge.

'We will take a short rest,' he announced. 'I will light a small fire and you can brew some coffee while I rub down the horses.'

'Rub down the horses? Why?' she asked, with some fear of seeming ignorant.

'A horse must warm up before it runs and cool down afterwards … despite the cold weather. We don't want, them overheated. Rubbin' gets their temperature back down to normal, coolin' off is important for relaxin' a horse's muscles and gettin' their heartrate to a good pace,' Anton calmly explained. 'You haven't been around horses much, huh?'

'Not too much. My pa always took care of them, and in San Francisco we didn't ride too much,' she explained.

Within minutes, flames were flickering. As he tended the horses, Kozlov glanced at the Lieutenant's intended bride. She busied herself by the fire, and the dancing light turned her hair into burnished gold. He took his eyes away.

'Mr Glanton must have owed you an awfully big favor,' Lucy remarked as they sipped coffee on either side of the little fire.

'We were in the army once — sort of — at least he was, and I worked as a scout,' Anton said. 'He was wounded, and I managed to drag him to cover. Reuben believes I saved his life.'

'So you weren't part of the army, but worked for them?' she pursued.

'Just as a scout, not officially part of the array, least not here.'

'Were you in the army back in your home country?'

'I was … '

There was silence between them.

'Why did you get out of the army, Anton?' she asked conversationally.

There was another more awkward silence, longer this time. Anton stared into the flames. He remembered other flames, not cooking fires but hungry tongues consuming the dry walls of Indian lodges. He kept looking into the flickering glow as the memories flooded back on a dark, evil tide. Once again, he heard screaming — frantic, terrible screams torn from the lips of women and children. There was gunfire, too, incessant, rolling thunder punctuated by the cries of the dying. And after gunfire came the ruthless rape of the young women who were still alive. He closed his eyes. His fingers clenched the coffee cup.

'I had my reasons, both here and at home, ma'am,' Kozlov said softly.

★ ★ ★

They were deep into the Northern Paiute country. Their territory covered parts of the Oregon territory, California, Idaho and Nevada.

The Paiute people were a nomadic tribe in a constant search for food through the forests of the mountains to the desert areas to the west. Hunting was not a skill that the Paiute men were able to master. Bows and arrows were the primary tool used, however, their bows were not very effective. Since the amount of animals they were able to kill was minimal, tribe members wore very little hide clothing. The Paiute were not rich in material items such as jewelry, clothes or art. Their nomadic lifestyle forced them to keep their goods to a minimum. Because they had so few possessions, they were not often the target of attacks from other tribes.

Just before noon, with the sun directly overhead, the prairie rose to low, rolling ridges. Some were wooded. Others were bald, starkly etched against the azure-colored sky. The riders kept their faces west, mounting one grassy hillock after another as the afternoon shadows lengthened.

It was close on dark when Kozlov chose

a place to camp. He drew rein beside a bed of stiff, brown reeds. The creek was hardly flowing, just a few iced over pools joined by a thin trickle of running water.

Anton sat saddle for a few moments to look around at the sheltering trees, and then he dismounted.

'Anton ... '

'Yes, ma'am?' the mountain man replied.

'I could use a wash,' she said.

He appraised her briefly and then said, 'You can heat up some water soon as we set up.'

Lucy Doniphon hesitated.

'And where will you be, Mr Kozlov?'

'Close by, but not too close, ma'am. I will tend the horses,' he said simply.

'After that,' she declared, 'I will fix us some supper.'

'There is grub in my saddlebag, ma'am,' Anton informed her. The frontiersman's eyes followed her as she climbed down from her tired mare. He began to build a cigarette. 'There is somethin' I have been meanin' to ask.'

'Sure, ask away, Mr Kozlov,' she invited, conscious that his eyes were still on her.

'How come a fine-lookin' woman like you needed to find a husband through a matrimonial agency?'

She smiled at the veiled compliment.

'Just curious ... ah hell, it ain't none of my business,' Anton added with a shrug.

'It is a long story, Mr Kozlov,' she said on her way to the creek.

He led the horse away, and when he glanced back, he glimpsed Lucy bending to dip water from the creek. She reminded him of his late wife, Lesya. He turned his attention to Socks and began to rub the horse down. They had made good time today, better than he had anticipated. After the first hour, Lucy had adjusted to Fleabag's lazy gait. He lit a second cigarette. Quite suddenly, Anton became aware that there were absolutely no sounds. Standing tall between Socks and the old nag, Fleabag, he let his eyes rest on the bare trees and the brown brush. He looked at their backtrail. Nothing moved. Removing the cigarette from his lips, Kozlov raised his eyes to the bald, slab of a ridge above them.

He saw three hatted riders etched against the sundown.

They were watching the woman. Slowly, he lifted his Hawken rifle from its saddle scabbard. The riders hadn't budged. Their eyes were fixed on Lucy Doniphon.

Casually, Anton shouldered his muzzle-loading rifle. He walked around the horses and headed to where he had left the saddles. He glanced at the ridge. The riders were drifting away.

Anton edged towards the reeds, parting them with his left hand. Lucy Doniphon was just out of his reach.

'Ma'am,' he said softly.

She gave him a startled look.

'Mr Kozlov!' she exclaimed. 'I was just getting the water ... '

'Ma'am, we have company.'

'Dear God — ' she began fearfully.

'Do exactly as I say. Get right into the

reeds and stay there. Do it now, ma'am.' There was a seriousness to his voice. She did as she was instructed.

'Yes, of course … '

Kozlov parted the reeds and looked cautiously around at the dusky wilderness. Nothing moved in the gray, silent stillness. He waited. The sharp snag of a twig made him look north. Holding his rifle with both hands, he watched the wooded slope.

It was almost dark when two riders slipped out of the trees like ghosts.

Sylvester Earhart seemed to dwarf his wiry roan. Just behind him came Nim Larkin, carrying two rifles. The unseen third rider would be Dutton Tully. The trader had decided to pursue his prey — as he had feared — and to get back at Anton Kozlov.

Kozlov turned his head to look for Dutton Tully. Moments later, he found him.

'Well now, look who we got here, boys!' Tully yelled. 'A purty little lady all alone in the wilderness and lookin' for company!'

'Where is the sidewinder who stole her away from us?' Earhart demanded, riding warily downslope towards the creek. 'I want that joker dead!'

Kozlov raised his Hawken rifle as Tully edged his gelding forward.

'If we go for the gal, I bet we will flush that sidewinder out,' Tully predicted.

Kozlov's rifle spat fire from the reed bed. The bullet smashed into Tully's chest at close range. Spewing blood, Tully screamed as he clung to his gelding's tangled mane. He tried to level his own rifle, but his lungs filled with blood and he crashed headlong into the grass. Two bullets slashed through the reeds. One whistled past Anton's left ear, the other kicked mud into his face. Nim Larkin loomed out of the dusky grayness. Still crouched, Kozlov aimed at the oncoming rider and squeezed his trigger. The horse reared, and Larkin slapped both hands to his bloody face and slid lifelessly out of the saddle.

Lucy Doniphon's frantic scream

sounded above the uproar.

Sylvester Earhart marched deliberately to the water's edge and grabbed for Lucy, dragging her out of hiding. Anton leveled his rifle without a word. Earhart cursed as he released the woman and aimed his Colt .45.

When he fired, the lead scorched Kozlov's arm. The frontiersman kept coming as Earhart raised his gun again and fired a second time. Lucy lurched against the trader, spoiling his aim. The bullet winged wide and smacked against a distant tree trunk.

Seizing the moment, Anton fired his Hawken rifle. Sylvester Earhart collapsed without a sound and lay still on the ground in a pool of his own blood.

'The other bank, Mr Kozlov!' Lucy Doniphon cried out. desperately.

Dutton Tully was still alive and had raised himself on his elbows. His face was contorted, and blood welled from his mouth. His fingers made a trembling claw around his gun.

Anton triggered, and the bullet struck

Tully neatly between his glassy eyes. Tully flopped face down like a discarded rag doll.

'Thanks, ma'am,' Anton said to Lucy, calmly.

Sobbing and shaking, Lucy clung to him and averted her eyes from the dead men.

'Mr Kozlov,' she whispered fearfully, 'you are bleeding.'

'Anton, please,' he said, looking down on his wound. 'I reckon the lead passed right on through.'

Blood dripped down his arm to his outstretched fingers, and red drops fell to the grass.

'All the same, it will need cleaning and bandaging, Mr K ... Anton,' she said firmly.

Anton looked down at his arm again. His torn shirt was soaked.

'Well, maybe you are right about that.'

'I am,' she assured him.

Lucy collected sticks and lit a small fire.

Anton sat beside the flames, nursing

his throbbing arm as she fetched water from the creek. With the water heating, he began to unbutton his shirt. The garment slipped easily away from his shoulder, but the fabric was matted to the wound.

'Here, let me help,' she offered.

She squatted beside him. Her hair brushed against his chest as she held his wounded arm in one hand and used the other to slowly peel away the strands of blood-soaked shirt from the two bullet holes where the slug had bored in and out of his flesh. She tore two strips from her petticoat and soaked one strip in the warm water and bathed his arm. Fleetingly, she let her eyes stray to his naked, muscular chest. Despite his advanced age, he was still fairly fit. Then she used the second strip of petticoat to bandage his wound.

'Thank you kindly, ma'am,' Anton said. He nodded at the darkness wreathing the slope to the creek. 'Now I have a chore to do. While you fix supper, I will dispose of those hard cases … and give you time to have that wash.'

'OK ... I mean, yes, Mr Kozlov,' she agreed.

'And please call me Anton or Old Moscow ... enough of the Mr Kozlov,' he said with a slight grin.

She nodded.

Anton dragged the three bodies to a cut bank on the outside of the creek and simply caved it in. Since it was too soon to return to camp, he sat himself on a log and rolled a smoke.

When he finally headed towards the glow of the campfire, he found Lucy bent over the cooking fire. Earlier, on the trail, he had shot a jack rabbit. The pieces had been rolled in flour and were frying now in the iron skillet.

'Smells real good, ma'am,' he said appreciatively.

'Lucy please, if I am going to call you Anton, you can call me by my name,' she replied.

'Sure,' he agreed.

'Great, hello, I am Lucy Doniphon,' she said, handing him his supper, 'but I have no idea what my real name is. Doniphon was the name my adopted parents gave me, and everyone called me Lucy since the time I could walk … I do not know why … but that is my name.'

'You were adopted?'

'Yes, but I was raised by a loving couple since the age of eight … or at least that was the age they believed me to be. My 'real' parents abandoned me either on purpose or for some other reason,' Lucy recalled. 'After that, I … just haven't thought about them.'

Anton started eating the rabbit.

'You have come a long way, Lucy,' he said.

Lucy watched him intently. Finally, hesitantly.

'Mr Kozlov … '

'I thought you wanted to use first names,' he said with a smirk.

She stared into her coffee.

'Anton, when I was fifteen or so, I committed a crime.' She looked up sharply. 'I … killed a man.' Her voice was husky and broken as her eyes held his. 'The gutter rat tried to rape me, so — so I used my knife. At first, I thought the judge was going to hang me, but instead he sentenced me to prison. Before long, I was farmed out to a man named Ellsworth Burrows.' Her breasts heaved against the fresh blouse she had put on, and she fell silent again for a few long moments. 'Burrows was married, and while Cathy Burrows was alive, I worked around the house. Then, a couple of years ago, Cathy died of pneumonia. Even before his wife's body was cold in the grave, Ellsworth Burrows tried to lay his hands on me. Those last two years with him were a living hell.' She poured coffee for Anton. 'After serving my full sentence, to the very last day, I walked free with nothing but the clothes on my back. Burrows was supposed to give me some money. All he did was slam the door in my face.' There were tears in her eyes. 'Like most women, I dreamt of a husband, home and family, but who would want Ellsworth Burrows' bed-warmer? No decent man, for sure!' She wiped her wet eyes with the back of her hand. 'Then I saw the notice in the newspaper, about wives for westerners.'

'So, you applied?'

'I figured it was my chance to start a new life,' she said, wiping away tears.

Anton finished his rabbit and asked one more question: 'And does your future husband know all of this?'

'No,' she said quickly and simply. 'The agency tells all its gentlemen clients they will be marrying well-bred ladies. When I questioned this with Mr McShane, he told me not to worry. He said women are in such short supply on the frontier that my husband-to-be will be so pleased to see me he won't care about anything else.'

Anton Kozlov regarded her over his coffee cup.

'I am sure the lieutenant will be real happy when he sees you.'

'I certainly hope so,' Lucy said. 'However, I am going to look for an opportunity to tell him the truth, just as I have told you.'

'Better get some shut-eye, Lucy,'

Anton advised.

He finished his coffee and went to check the horses. He looked back at the fire and saw her slim, shapely figure in the flickering glow. As he observed, he thought of his late wife, and watched as Lucy hugged her knees in the fire's warmth. He liked her — and admired her. She had been in life's cesspool and she was making an effort to haul herself out. He had a lot of time for a woman like that. When he returned to the camp, he walked around the fire and draped a blanket over her shoulder.

'Thank you, Anton.'

'I thought I told you to get some sleep?'

She looked earnestly at the old mountain man.

'Anton, tell me about Lieutenant Judd Reed.'

He looked at her. 'I thought you had been writin' to him.'

'We wrote two letters each, that was all,' Lucy told him. 'A woman can hardly get to know her man through a couple of letters.'

Anton sat down by the fire and poured himself a second cup of coffee. 'What do you want to know?' he asked finally.

'Does he look handsome? How would you describe his look?' she asked hopefully.

'Well, the lieutenant … Judd … is tall and heavy-set and several years younger than me,' Anton said guardedly.

'I imagine he will be a fine figure of a man in his uniform,' she said wistfully.

He shrugged. 'That is for you to decide.'

'I guess he is a man used to giving and receiving orders,' Lucy said pensively. 'I will need to fit in with his chosen career.'

'Yeah, I reckon,' Anton said, building another cigarette.

'Please tell me more about him,' Lucy urged.

'It is a long trail to Devil's Canyon,' Kozlov said. 'We will have plenty of time to talk.'

She nodded and settled down beside the fire.

'I will try hard to be a good wife,' she vowed.

Anton lit his cigarette in the fire's glowing embers as he said, 'I am sure you will.'

'Judd is your friend,' Lucy said, finally closing her eyes, 'so I am sure of one thing — he must be a nice man — like you. Good night, Anton Kozlov.'

He smoked the cigarette down as she fell asleep.

Placing his rifle within easy reach, he leaned back against his saddle. Tonight, Anton 'Old Moscow' Kozlov would not sleep. He would listen, keep watch and drink coffee. From time to time, his eyes would grow heavy and he would turn his attention to keeping them open. He would make sure nothing, or no one disturbed the woman's sleep tonight.

He buttoned his coat.

It was going to be a long night for him.

★ ★ ★

They broke camp before first light and rode west into the silent wilderness. They crossed a muddy flat and mounted a gradual slope which rose to a lonely, jagged crest.

The sun was up when they reached the top. They sat saddle for a few minutes to rest the horses and look over the country they would cross. The wind began to increase.

A long, uneven plateau of a broad expanse of sage-brush lay below them, and then the lesser slopes of the ranges. Anton pointed out the pass they would take, and Lucy silently nodded.

Kozlov nudged his sorrel forward. He was leading Dutton Tully's shaggy gelding. The horses belonging to the other dead men, had run off during the shooting.

They were less than half way to the plateau when Anton drew rein sharply.

'What is it?' Lucy asked.

'Smoke,' he said, 'comin' from the mouth of the pass.'

'Is it from Indians?' she asked anxiously.

'No, reckon not,' he told her. 'It is just smoke risin'. Somethin' is burnin'.'

She strained to look but saw only faint glimpses of the smoke. 'What do you think it could be?'

Anton appraised the yawning entrance to the pass. 'We will know when we get there, I reckon. Probably be around noon time.'

The tall grass brushed their legs as they headed away from the jagged ridge. They crossed a frozen river and picked their way through a field of weathered boulders. Two hours slipped by without much notice. They rested in a dry wash, not far from the bare bones of a deer. Kozlov studied the smoke. It had spread into a thin, flimsy haze which almost concealed the pass. The sun climbed higher and scorched the plateau as Anton led Lucy onward. The haze began to lift. Now Anton could only make out thin ribbons of smoke.

The plateau was breaking up. Ravines

and canyons cut huge fissures into the prairie.

The noonday sun displayed the wilderness with unshadowed clarity.

Just ahead, the pass gaped like a toothless mouth. Anton lifted his rifle from the saddle scabbard as he mounted the slope. He glimpsed a single curl of smoke drifting skywards. He halted Socks and waited for Lucy to draw rein beside him.

'Keep close,' he advised, with his eyes on the smoke.

He rode slowly, threading through another patch of boulders. They mounted a steep slope and came upon wagon tracks. They followed the tracks for a few more yards and stopped. Lucy was so close to Anton that their horses touched.

'Dear God!' she whispered fearfully.

Just a few paces away, in the pass itself, lay the blackened skeleton of a wagon. The charred remains of the conveyance had a distinctive curved floor and once a canvas cover that arched — now smoldering strips — over the charred, wooden hoops, lay on its side. The Conestoga wagon would have been horse-drawn. Twisted wheels faced the sun. A piano had been thrown to the ground, and a solitary ribbon of smoke rose slowly from its glowing flame. A shaggy goat and a mongrel dog lay sprawled side by side, with arrows protruding from their seared carcasses. Fragments of furniture, hacked and splintered, were strewn haphazardly over the fire-blasted wreckage. He could smell roasted flesh. He could smell death.

'Stay here, Lucy,' he said tersely.

He slid from his saddle.

Holding his rifle firmly in both hands, he edged up to the wagon. The ground was hot under his boots. A gust of wind made the piano frame light up like a lantern. For a long moment, Anton stood motionless. His keen, penetrating eyes looked deep into the pass. They roved along the steep-sided walls, lingering on two dark caves which stared back at him like eyeless sockets. He studied the flat in front of the pass and then checked their back trail. He saw no movement.

Cautiously, he walked to the dead animals.

The smell of burnt flesh became stronger. He glanced back at Lucy. She sat her horse obediently, white-faced and trembling. Kozlov edged warily around the other side of the wagon. There were three bodies, pinned to the underside of the Conestoga by long lances. Two were men. Both had been scalped but one had strands of singed silver hair hanging like string from his chin. The woman was in between the two men. Anton knew who they were. He had spoken to them as he had come into Bear Creek Pass. Looking around, Anton saw Maude's baby. The tiny body had been crushed by falling furniture.

Anton Kozlov picked up a feathered arrow and examined its markings.

His searching eyes found the tracks left by unshod ponies. Studying them closely, Kozlov figured there had been five, maybe six warriors. He frowned at the tracks and glanced back at the blackened corpses. This was no war party, he concluded. It looked more like young bucks sent out to hunt. They had found the settlers, and things had got out of hand apparently.

'Anton ... ' Lucy called anxiously.

'Stay there!' he told her. 'You don't want to see this.'

'Are they ... ?'

'Yes ... all dead,' Anton told her solemnly.

It was then that he saw the rider.

The solitary Indian had just mounted a long, curving rim that presided over the pass. Motionless on his wiry pinto, he watched Anton and the girl. Acting as if he had not noticed the Indian, Anton walked slowly around the wagon. He glimpsed another brave edging his paint pony under the low branches of a towering pine just inside the pass.

'Half a dozen Indians attacked the wagon and butchered the family,' Anton said when he returned to Lucy. 'At least two of the lousy polecats are watchin' us as we speak,' he added as he eased himself casually into the saddle.

Holding the rifle with one hand, he gathered the reins in the other.

'Don't look,' he warned. 'If they think we have seen them, they might come for us right away.'

'What do we do?' she whispered.

'We will try to give them the slip,' Anton said as a coyote yipped from their back trail. It was a human coyote. 'First, we will ride over to those trees.'

'The big pines?' Lucy asked.

'Yes,' Anton said. 'Ride slowly, like there is nothin' wrong,' he instructed.

'I will be right beside you,' she promised fervently.

He nudged Socks into a walk. He was sure the Indians had spotted Lucy. They would doubtless try to capture this auburn-haired prize. He glimpsed another Indian rider, a lean, bronze streak, coming out of a thicket. The human coyote yipped again and was answered by another. Anton and Lucy made the pines and slipped between two tall trunks. The needled branches made a green canopy over their heads as Anton struck due south, away from the pass. They rode fast now, weaving between the pines. Emerging from the trees, they headed across a flat ridge top overshadowed by another, steeper rise. Still with the rifle in his hand, Anton led the way up the incline. It would have meant suicide to go through the pass, but this trail was longer. Judd would have to wait an extra day for his bride.

They reached the bare crest of the rise. The wind caught them and took away their breath. Anton guided Socks under a rock ledge.

'Have we shaken them off?' Lucy asked hopefully.

'Perhaps.'

'You don't sound too certain,' she noted.

'Fellers like that are taught to read sign as soon as they can talk and walk,' Anton explained to her. 'Readin' a trail is as natural as breathin', to an Indian buck.'

'So, they could be right behind us?'

Her look was one of fear.

'I intend to find out,' Anton stated.

Motioning her to remain silent, he took two swigs from his canteen and then slipped from his saddle. He climbed the ledge and stood under a stunted tree to look over their back trail. He watched and waited patiently. Ten minutes later, he saw five riders emerging from a thicket. They were so far away that they looked like ants. There they were, relentlessly following the trail.

Anton shouldered his Hawken rifle and returned to his horse.

'They are an hour or so behind us,' he announced. 'They don't look to be in any particular rush because they know we will have to rest. That is when they will try to take us.'

Terror showed on Lucy's face. 'So — so we will have to fight them?'

'I reckon ... looks to be that way,' Anton said, remounting his sorrel, Socks. 'But I am goin' to choose the place for sure.'

They kept riding as the shadows stretched and a sudden storm swept the high country. The gale portion of the storm lasted over an hour, then down came the blessed sleet and snow all through the night and the next day, the rain and wind alternating and blending in the valley.

They kept riding when the clouds vanished, and the dying sun retreated to the western escarpments. The snowy skirts of the mountains appeared beneath the lifting fringes of the clouds, and the sun shone out through colored windows, producing one of the most glorious after-storm effects. It was close to sundown when Kozlov found the clearing in the pine forest. He left Lucy with the horses as he walked slowly around the trees which hemmed them in.

'Build a fire, would ya, Lucy?' he asked.

'Is that a good idea? A fire?' she repeated incredulously.

Anton nodded his confirmation. 'Yes, make it a real big one.'

He tethered the horses. Dusk clothed the forest as Lucy gathered sticks and started a fire burning. The flames were already leaping high as Anton returned with two saddles and blankets.

'Anton, won't the fire attract the Indians?' Lucy looked unsure.

He nodded. 'That's right.'

She looked confused. 'Then why_'

'Throw more wood on the fire, Lucy. I want a real bonfire goin'.' He smiled at the woman. She did not return it.

He lumped the saddles together on to the ground. Then he bunched blankets over the saddle rolls to give the impression that they covered sleeping bodies. Taking off his Stetson, he placed it over one saddle horn. While Lucy watched with anticipation, he put two coffee cups on the ground. Satisfied with the deception tactic, he picked up his spare rifle.

He looked to Lucy with a seriousness. 'You know how to use this?' he asked.

'Yeah ... I mean ... I reckon I do,' she said. 'It is the one thing I learned from Ellsworth Burrows.'

'Here,' he replied. 'Put the coffee pot in the embers and come with me.'

He walked to the nearest fallen pine tree, and she joined him behind the mossy trunk. He leaned his rifle against the tree and checked his six-gun. The wind rose. The fire spat and leapt.

'These diggers will be surprised,' Anton said.

Lucy looked perplexed. 'Diggers?'

'A lot of people called the Paiute 'diggers' as they have a practice of diggin' for roots for food,' Anton explained. 'The trap is baited,' he added softly. 'Now lay flat so the trunk shields us. When they get here, they will figure we are fast asleep by the fire. When they come in for the kill, they will be right in the firelight. We have to make every bullet count, Lucy, you understand?'

She nodded reluctantly.

He eased himself down so that he lay full length on his side. She slid beside him, facing him in the gathering twilight. He could feel the softness and warmth of her body. It wasn't the first time that the thought of her reminded him of his Lesya. Lieutenant Reed was a very lucky man. Almost a full hour passed. The fire glow was intense, flaring almost, to the edge of the clearing. A red-eyed marmot scampered across the clearing and disappeared into the darkness.

Anton Kozlov reached for his rifle.

Flat to the ground, he waited as the night fell utterly silent.

Then he heard the sharp whinny of a pony and the crunch of a hoof on dead wood. Beside him, Lucy Doniphon clutched her rifle. Branches rustled on the other side of the clearing.

Slowly, Anton edged himself up, just high enough to see over the fallen tree.

At first, all he could see was the fire glow surrounded by a rim of darkness. Finally, pine boughs parted. The ruddy glow framed the face of a Paiute brave. He was dressed in a breechcloth with leather leggings and buckskin shirt. There was no war bonnet. The Indian appraised the camp slowly. Then he dropped silently from the back of his pony. Another warrior hovered on the edge with a knife between his teeth. Two more sat their horses, watching, still in the saddle as they emerged warily from the night.

The Paiute Indian who had appeared first, still stared fixedly at the two blanket-covered shapes. He held a bow and arrow. Suddenly, a fearsome war cry rose from his lips, and the raiders surged into the clearing for the kill. The warrior who had crawled into the clearing reared up with fire glinting on his steel blade.

The knife plunged ferociously into the bunched blankets.

Stabbing wildly, the Paiute brave stared in baffled rage as the blankets fell away.

'Shoot to kill!' Anton commanded as the bewildered Paiute jerked his knife free and yelled a frenzied warning.

Anton's first bullet blasted into the brave at the bedrolls, cutting short his cry of anger. Screaming with rage and realizing they had ridden into a trap, the mounted warriors pulled hard on their reins while those on foot halted in their tracks. Kozlov beaded the leading rider as Lucy grappled with the other gun. Two rifles boomed in rapid succession. Anton's bullet hammered into the nearest warrior, ripping into his left lung. Spewing blood, the brave tried desperately to wheel his terrified pony. The effort was too much, and he fell with a dull, lifeless thud. Lucy's bullet struck the other rider, shattering his shoulder. Suddenly a tomahawk sliced into the log, just inches from Lucy's face. Then a bullet kicked wood splinters between Anton and Lucy as they leveled their rifles once more. The Paiute was framed in the firelight as he squinted into the darkness. His next shot went well over Kozlov's head, and then Anton took careful aim and fired. Dead on his feet, the Paiute buckled at the knees, dropped and then sprawled into the fire.

The corpse snuffed Lucy's bonfire to smoking embers.

There was a long, eerie, uncomfortable silence. Three Northern Paiute braves lay dead in the smoky half-light. The others had vanished into the night.

They heard the snap of dry twigs and the muffled sound of hoofs in pine needles.

'They are gone!' Lucy said, almost relieved.

'Stay right here,' Anton advised.

'But — '

He gave her a stern look. 'They won't leave their dead behind,' he told her. 'They need to bury them with their possessions.'

'So, they will be back?'

'They believe ghosts could remain in this world and plague the livin', unless properly buried and prayers offered,' Anton explained.

'OK, how soon?' Lucy asked.

'Real soon,' he murmured. 'What you are hearin' is an old Indian trick. Slap a couple of ponies into a trot to make it sound like they have gone, and then come back on foot.'

They waited in the silence.

Blood and body fat from the Paiute brave who had fallen into the fire hissed in the embers. The shrill whinny of a pony came like a shriek in the night. Anton's Hawken rifle grew cold in his hands. Lucy sat with her back to the tree trunk.

There was a sudden rustle in the darkness, and then the braves reared out of the night, with tomahawks and spears raised. Anton's Hawken rifle thundered at point blank range, blasting a bullet into a lean, bronze chest. The Paiute warrior swayed on the balls of his feet as blood gushed down his belly. He plunged forward, collapsing over the fallen tree beside Anton. The other brave reached for Lucy. Her gun boomed and the bullet ripped into the warrior's groin. He bore her to the ground with the weight of his body, and a glinting tomahawk flashed in the last light from the fading embers. The lethal blade thudded into the ground inches from her face, chopping off some of her flowing hair. Anton fired twice into the Paiute's back, snapping his spine like matchwood. The frontiersman set aside his smoking rifle and dragged the lifeless figure off Lucy. She scrambled to her feet, sobbing violently, and tumbled into Anton's arms. He let her cling to him for a full minute before he reached behind his neck to unclasp her hands.

'We will find another place to make camp,' he whispered softly.

4

The Late Arrival of Lt. Reed's Bride-to-Be

The overhang had the rank smell of animals, but none were currently in residence. The ceiling was high enough to admit the horses, and the shelter was sufficient for concealment.

Anton Kozlov carefully stoked the small fire well back in the rear of the cave. This was another night when he would not sleep. He looked across the fire at Lucy. Exhausted by her ordeal, she was still awake under a blanket. Their eyes met and held in the fire glow. They had shared terrible danger and seen violent death. There was a bond between the two of them now.

'You can sleep safely,' Anton assured her.

'I'm not sure that I could sleep,' she

said. 'Not that I don't feel safe with you here.'

'We move out at first light,' he said. 'I am hopin' those five Paiute braves were just out on their own, but you can never be sure about a tiling like that. How's the coffee pot?' he asked.

She looked at the pot. 'Just about empty. I will fix us some fresh brew,' Lucy declared.

'You need to get some sleep,' he told her directly.

'First, I will make more coffee,' Lucy said firmly, pulling the blanket, from her body. 'It is the least I can do before I sleep, with you staying awake to keep watch, wouldn't you agree?'

Anton Kozlov did not reply.

The fire flickered as Lucy attended to the coffee pot. She looked extraordinarily beautiful in the ruddy glow. Her hair hung free. Her breasts made a delicious swell against her blouse. He was old, but not dead. He had thoughts of his Lesya. He watched as she slid the coffee pot back into the embers. Then she stood up and walked around the fire. She squatted down in front of him and with her hands, cupped his face that was flush with stubble now. For a moment, her lips hovered just inches from his mouth...oh, to kiss Lesya one more time.

'Good night, Anton Kozlov,' she whispered.

She pressed her soft lips to his right cheek, lingering there. Slowly, seemingly with reluctance, she stood up and returned to her side of the fire. Saying nothing more, she retrieved her blanket and wrapped its warmth around her body. She closed her eyes.

Kozlov watched as she drifted into sleep. She was the kind of woman most men would be proud to wed. He hoped his former stepson would appreciate Lucy Doniphon.

The next day dawned cold and gray. They ate a quick breakfast and headed into the early-morning mist. Keeping to the timbered slopes, they pushed west over the mountains, and made camp that night by a windswept lake.

Much of the rock that surrounded the area around them was granite or a near relative of granite. There were dividing bands of heat and pressure-altered sedimentary rock_or all that was left of a once extensive sedimentary basin_and some large areas of old volcanic rock, that had ejected out of the earth's surface long before they had traversed them.

It was close to noon two days later that Kozlov saw Indian signs.

Two signals rose into the air against the snow-capped peak. Reining Socks, he read their message. Braves were being summoned. More smoke puffs were sucked into the sky from a ridge to the east. Anton picked the trail even more cautiously as the afternoon wore on. Just before sundown, he motioned Lucy to draw her mare into the shelter of three jagged rocks. Signaling her not to speak, he sat saddle and waited. Soon a big bunch of mounted Paiute Indians filtered through the pines down trail. Kozlov counted fifteen warriors, all painted for war. He waited a long time before resuming the trail under a watery moon.

That same night, there was no fire. By first light, they were crossing a timbered ridge. Halfway through the morning, they came upon the tracks of unshod ponies. More than a dozen riders had passed less than an hour earlier.

Because they had been forced to take the longer trail, there would be two more days and nights before they reached the end of their journey. The first of those days went without incident. On the last day, however, they came across the charred shell of a cabin. Its burnt timbers were still warm, and the old trapper's remains were a sight which Kozlov quietly concealed from Lucy.

An hour later, Anton spotted two warriors building a fire. He and Lucy circled them and took an old deer trail which twisted down to a shallow river. They crossed under the cover of darkness and mounted the long, steady slope which stretched to the rim. It was here, crossing the curved balcony rim that they glimpsed distant lanterns.

'Devil's Canyon,' he said simply. 'You will see the man you are goin' to marry at sun-up.'

★ ★ ★

They came into the canyon just as the swirling mist began to lift. Riding down the wooded slope with Lucy looking eagerly ahead, Anton saw the basin for the first time after the long, dangerous journey. The north wind which had howled and whistled all night, now dropped to a cold whisper. Anton saw steers grazing on the frosty grass.

It seemed as if the settlers of Devil's Canyon were ignorant to any likelihood of danger. Maybe no one had spotted the distant smoke signals. Perhaps the Paiute Indians had not ranged this far west.

They passed Burt Roberts' place, a sprawling log house still shrouded in mist. The Reverend Burt Roberts, now into his late fifties, had been one of the first settlers to claim this canyon. Three times married, the bearded giant was probably still in bed with his latest wife, plump Henrietta, who was more than twenty years his junior.

On a lonely ridge overlooking the river, they heard the thud of an ax splitting wood. Will Alvord was cutting firewood. His wife, Crazy Jane, stood on the front step of their ramshackle cabin with her hands on her hips. She was a half-breed Paiute.

Anton could see his own cabin now, on the far side of the creek.

He glanced down canyon at three other cabins. Dave Calhoun's stone and log place was sheltered by a pine grove. Calhoun kept to himself. Some said he used to ride the owl hoot trail from time to time. Grayson Weathers and his young wife, Clara, owned the next spread, and beyond their lands, Jed Bliss had built a soddy. Canyon talk said that Bliss was another with an Indian squaw to warm his bed.

Anton slowed his sorrel, Socks.

He looked briefly south, past all the cabins to the dark, high walls of the stockade. It was the outpost the soldiers had raised well before the canyon was settled. They called it the last outpost west. A couple of years later, Fort Bighorn was built, and the stockade relinquished. The blue-coats had wanted to burn it to the ground, but a deputation of newly-arrived settlers persuaded Major Amos Peabody to leave it standing. They figured the stockade could be useful in the event of an Indian raid.

The two riders splashed across the creek.

Riding the narrow track which led to Anton's land, they saw five horses tethered outside his cabin. Smoke curled from his chimney, and a soldier lounged near the door. The front door had been carelessly left open, and Anton's mongrel dog was tied to a post. Lieutenant Judd Reed and his men had obviously made themselves at home. Anton Kozlov was angry, but he decided to keep his annoyance in check. He didn't want to spoil this moment for Lucy Doniphon.

'Anton,' she said as they rode closer, 'I am scared.'

'Of the lieutenant? There is no reason to be,' he offered.

'What if he doesn't like me?' she asked anxiously.

'No chance of that,' the old mountain man assured her.

The soldier at the door saw their approach. He straightened and called the men inside. Two more soldiers ambled out of the cabin. Anton and Lucy headed across the last stretch of waving grass. Another trooper emerged from the cabin, followed closely by Judd.

Shrugging into his blue tunic, he pushed his way through his men and stood with arms folded, awaiting the two riders.

'There he is, Lucy,' Anton announced as they rode closer. 'Lieutenant in the United States Army, cavalry trooper, and your future husband, Judd Reed.'

'He — looks a fine man,' Lucy said as they slowed their mounts.

They rode between the two towering spruce trees which dwarfed the cabin. They moved around a small vegetable patch. Finally, with the dog barking a welcome, they drew rein half a dozen paces from the cabin.

For a long moment, Judd's eyes raked his young bride. Then he gave a satisfied grin. His expression changed when he looked at his stepfather.

'You are late with my woman!'

Anton exhaled. 'Yeah, we ran into some trouble.'

The trooper turned his eyes to Anton. 'What kinda trouble?'

'Double trouble, Judd,' Anton said. 'We will talk inside.'

'First,' Judd announced, taking some folded notes from his tunic pocket, 'I will pay you the fifty bucks you are owed.'

'I reckon that first you ought to help Lucy down,' Anton suggested. 'She has been a long time in the saddle.'

Ignoring that advice, Judd walked stiffly up to the horse.

'I don't like owing any man,' he said,

shoving the bank notes into his former stepfather's hand. 'And that includes you, Old Moscow.'

'Since you have taken over my cabin,' Anton observed coldly, 'I hope the coffee's hot.'

'Been hot for over a day,' Trooper Hal Yacey muttered.

Anton eased himself out of the saddle while the grinning, soon-to-be groom walked casually to Lucy's horse.

'Well, well, so you are the woman they sent me,' Judd Reed said approvingly. 'You are sure worth the twenty bucks I paid to that agency!'

'Thank you,' she said pleasantly. 'I think.'

Judd reached up and clapped a possessive hand on her left arm.

'Old Moscow here says I oughta lift you down, Lucy,' Judd said, his fingers biting into her flesh. 'I reckon he is right.'

Anton looped his reins around a hitching post. The four troopers stood grinning as Lucy put her hands tentatively on her future husband's thick shoulders, Judd's big hands found her waist and he lifted her clean out of the saddle. The burly blue-coat lowered her until her feet touched the ground. He did not release her. In fact, he clutched her hard to his heavy body. He crushed so tightly that she could barely breathe.

Finally, Judd relaxed his grip. Lucy stepped back from his bear-like embrace.

'I have been looking forward to meeting you,' she said, smiling.

'You sure are a sight for sore eyes, and you feel good too,' Judd said as she flushed scarlet and the trooper snickered. 'Now let's see if you know how to look after a man's stomach! We haven't eaten since supper last night, so you can rustle us up some grub. The stove's hot, and there is a frying pan … '

'Hold on, Judd,' Anton interrupted. 'Lucy's had one helluva long ride. She might need a rest before she starts on chores.'

'She is my woman, Anton,' the cavalry officer snapped. 'I know what is good for her.'

The two men exchanged heated glances.

'It is all right, Anton,' Lucy said. 'I need to show my future husband I am a good cook.'

Judd frowned because Lucy had called the old mountain man by his first name.

'Suit yourself,' Anton replied.

Anton walked into his home. He wasn't exactly given to tidiness, but he bristled at the way Judd's troop had turned his cabin into a pigsty. The place stank of stale tobacco. Unwashed plates, playing cards, discarded food and even dirty clothes littered the floor. Sparks must have fallen from the untended stove_the floorboards were charred.

'Sorry about the mess, Old Moscow, but you know how soldiers are,' Judd said offhandedly. 'You used to be one yourself.' Judd Reed folded his arms. 'I will get my woman to clean up the place for you.'

'I will take care of it myself, after you move out,' Anton Kozlov decided.

'I insist,' Reed said. 'It will be no trouble for the future Mrs. Judd Reed.'

'I told you no,' snapped Anton rather coldly.

'OK,' Judd shrugged as Lucy busied herself at the stove.

'Was your mission successful?' Anton asked, as he rolled a cigarette.

'Sure enough was,' Trooper Yacey said, as he slurped lukewarm coffee. 'We caught up with the yellow-bellied bastards.'

'And where are they now?' Anton asked.

'Six feet under,' Judd put in casually.

'More like a few feet under,' laughed Tuck Gravens.

'I thought you said you were takin' them back to face a court martial?' Anton pursued.

'I made a command decision,' Reed said crisply. 'We trailed them to a canyon. They had guns, and I wasn't about to risk the lives of four good soldiers here.'

'So you gunned them down?' asked Anton.

'We saved a lot of time and trouble,' Lieutenant Reed snapped.

Lucy began to fry venison steak in the pan. White-faced, she looked from Anton to the man she was set to marry. Judd's eyes had narrowed to twin slits, and his fleshy lips twitched nervously.

'It is army business, old man,' Judd said coldly.

'Like Old Bootleg Canyon?'

There was a long, icy silence. Lieutenant Judd Reed stared at the old mountain man who had once been married to his mother, briefly, and thrust a cigar between his lips. Trooper Yacey exchanged glances with Ben Copeland. There was a sneer on Tuck Gravens' lips. Alan Loomis looked bewildered at Anton's remark.

'Hurry up with that grub, woman,' Judd said irritably. 'We are all hungry men.'

'I am doing my best,' Lucy said as Judd kept his brooding eyes fixed on the old mountain man.

Anton walked to the stove and poured

himself some coffee.

'You said there were reasons why you were late,' Judd remarked.

'The stage never made Bear Creek Pass,' Anton explained. 'It was wrecked along the trail and the passengers walked to Sylvester Earhart's place. Earhart took a shine to your bride-to-be, and he came after us with some other hard cases. There was gunplay, and I had to bury them.'

'Anton risked his life for me, Judd,' Lucy said earnestly as she turned the steaks in the pan.

Judd ignored her and addressed Anton again.

'You said there was double trouble.'

'Yep … I did … Indians,' Anton said, sipping his coffee. The soldiers all listened intently now. 'They killed a wagonload of settlers travelin' alone and then came after the two of us.'

'Well, you made it, so I figure the Indians are now buzzard bait,' Judd said nonchalantly.

Anton nodded. 'I set a trap which they

rode right into.'

'So did you learn that from the United States Army or from your old Russian days?' Judd asked cuttingly.

Anton let the jibe pass. His eyes swept over the troopers, wiping the smirks from their faces. There was another long, cold silence.

'Let's just say your bride is here in one piece, Judd,' Anton said. 'Now it is your turn to look after her, Lieutenant.'

'Don't you worry none about that, Old Moscow,' Judd said, his eyes riveted on the woman.

'You will need to keep a sharp look-out on the trail to Fort Bighorn,' Anton advised. 'We saw more Indians on the way. The country we rode through was lousy with Paiute Indian sign.'

'We rode northwest chasing those yellow-bellied deserters, and we never saw a trace of Injuns,' Judd said disparagingly.

'Didn't even smell an Injun,' Trooper Yacey yawned.

'All the same, be careful,' Anton again

advised. 'You will have a woman with you.'

'Forget that, Old Moscow!' Judd snapped. 'You are finished with being concerned about my bride!'

Lucy served the venison steaks. The soldiers ate the meal, lounging around the table. Anton sat apart from the others. He drank a second cup of coffee as the troopers yarned, and Judd watched his bride like a hawk. Yellow-haired Copeland smelled of whiskey, and his breath was foul. Yacey was still slurping coffee. He thrust a cigar between his lips, just as he had done at Old Bootleg Canyon. Gravens looked half asleep. Loomis seemed different from the rest. Not only was he younger, but he seemed ill at ease.

'You men can go outside and get the horses ready for the trail,' Judd directed.

The troopers tramped outside, leaving the Lieutenant and the mountain man with Lucy.

Judd stubbed the ash of his cigar.

'Anton, we need to borrow your other room.'

Anton looked at the officer with confusion. 'What on earth for?'

'It is time for me and my lovely bride to get better acquainted,' Judd winked. 'Just ten minutes will be fine — for now.'

Lucy stepped back a few paces.

'Please, Judd, let's not rush things,' she said. 'I would rather ride to the fort, and — '

'Woman, I make the decisions!' Judd said flatly.

'No, Judd; in this house, I make them,' Anton declared.

'Dammit, Anton — '

'Lieutenant! Lieutenant Reed!' Hal Yacey's urgent, summons bellowed from the doorstep of the cabin.

'What in the living hell is up?' Judd Reed demanded irritably.

The trooper was excited. 'Smoke!'

Anton was outside first with the lieutenant bustling through the doorway moments later. The four cavalry troopers, bunched near their horses, were staring at the smoke signal rising from the northern slopes of the valley. The signal fire had probably been lit on the ridge where Anton had caught the old Paiute Indian, Looks at the Bear, stealing from his traps.

'What does it say, Old ... Anton?' Judd asked.

'It is war smoke.'

'Then we had best get into the saddle and ride,' Judd decided swiftly. 'We will need to inform Major Peabody.'

'You could ride through the valley,' Anton suggested to his soldier visitors as he watched the dark, ominous puffs. 'If there is a raid, the settlers could use five extra guns.'

'Judd, Anton's right,' Lucy pleaded with her future husband. 'The settlers will need help....'

'I will thank you to keep your opinions to yourself!' Judd Reed said tersely. 'This is army business, woman.'

'Hell!' Trooper Alan Loomis exclaimed, pointing to the western rim of Devil's Canyon. 'Two more smoke signals!'

Anton stepped into the yard. Two thin columns of white smoke were drifting in the sunlight. Suddenly the columns broke into separate puffs. He glanced south to the end of the canyon, beyond the old stockade. Three more signals were rising into the morning sky. He saw the wide eyes of young Trooper Loomis looking in the same direction. That was the way to Fort Bighorn. A lone signal puffed into the air from the sheer walls of Minaret's Pass.

'You won't be ridin' back to Fort Big-horn in a hurry,' Anton Kozlov informed them soberly. 'We are ringed in from the looks of the signals.'

'Bastards!' Yacey whispered hoarsely.

'They must have followed you here,' Judd muttered. 'You killed some braves, so the tribe wants blood. Dammit, you should have covered your tracks better, you old fool.'

Anton ran his eyes around the valley rims.

'They are not here on my account,' he

121

announced.

'Then — why?' Trooper Loomis stammered.

'Oh, probably just a murder raid,' Hal Yacey said, snatching his army carbine from its saddle scabbard.

'Chief Numaga signed a treaty,' Anton said. 'Somethin' bad must have happened to make them break it.'

'Treaty or no treaty, you can never trust those Snake Indians,' Judd muttered beside the mountain man.

'Snake? I thought they were Paiute?' Lucy whispered.

'One and the same,' answered Anton. 'Some people refer to them as the Snake Indians, for snakin' along rivers, I reckon.'

Once again, Anton looked around at the ring of slowly rising smoke. He strode to Socks and unsheathed his rifle.

'We canyon folk have a way of warnin' everyone else of danger,' Anton declared.

He lifted his rifle and aimed at the sky. Then he discharged his gun three times in rapid-fire succession. He waited as the echoes reverberated the whole length of the valley.

'By now, every settler should be outside his cabin checkin' what is up. I reckon everyone will see the smoke now.'

Three shots boomed from Roberts' place in acknowledgement of the warning. Gunfire came next from Calhoun's spread, followed immediately by blasts from Will Alvord. The echoes began to die, but then they heard from Weathers and Bliss.

'They all know to make for the stockade,' Anton explained.

'Mount up,' Judd told his troopers. He looked at Lucy then and added, 'You too, woman.'

'Are you going to help the settlers?' Lucy asked Judd anxiously.

Plainly angered by her question, Judd merely pointed to her horse and then stood waiting with his hands on hips as she walked to the horse and mounted. The four troopers made ready to ride.

'I told you what I intend to do,' Judd Reed said tersely. 'We are riding to inform Major Peabody of an Indian uprising.'

'I would not advise tryin' to get through the pass,' Anton said, watching a second smoke signal rise just south of the pass.

'I am in command, old man,' Judd said crisply. 'And I make the decisions.'

'To ride into that pass would be bookin' a ticket to the nearest cemetery,' Anton Kozlov warned.

'You were yellow in the army,' Judd sneered, 'and you are still yellow now!'

Anton's fist smashed into Judd's face like a hammer. Judd staggered back with blood gushing from his broken nose. He fell hard against his horse and then pitched forward into a barrage of blows — to his jaw, to his chest and straight at his gaping mouth. Two teeth sailed across the yard, and Judd Reed fell flat. When Anton looked up, he was facing four guns.

'Just say the word, Lieutenant,' Trooper Hal Yacey grated, looking down his rifle barrel at Anton's head.

'Judd!' Lucy screamed frantically. 'Don't do it! He is your friend!'

Judd eased himself painfully into a

kneeling position. Blood streamed down his face and soaked into his tunic. His chest heaved. Shaking with rage, he glared at the old mountain man. Still kneeling, he contemplated the arc of loaded guns aimed at Kozlov.

'Like she said, you are my friend,' Judd said indistinctly as he spat out another tooth. 'More important than that, you brought my bride to me. That is the only reason I am gonna tell my men to put their guns down.' The troopers lowered their rifles as Judd nursed his jaw. 'But listen — don't you ever lay a hand on me again, because next time I will have you shot down like a dog!' Judd swung into his saddle then. Possessively, he leaned over and took hold of Lucy's bridle. 'So long, Old Moscow.' Then he bellowed the order. 'Make for the pass!'

'You could be takin' your bride on a death ride,' Anton warned stubbornly.

'Her safety is my business and not yours, from now on.'

Anton watched them ride out.

Lucy stole a quick, desperate glance

over her shoulder. Judd said something, and she turned obediently to face him.

Signal smoke was still rising. Knowing that time could be running out, Anton hurried into his cabin and quickly began to stuff supplies into his saddlebag. Then he carried out an armful of pelts and roped them to the spare horse. He went back inside to replenish his ammunition and check his guns. Finally, he untied the old mongrel dog.

Although it probably wouldn't matter, he closed the cabin door.

Riding his sorrel and with the spare horse and the dog behind him, he set his face for the stockade.

5

Fire in the Canyon

'Shut the gate!' Anton Kozlov commanded.

He stood on the platform behind the north wall. From that elevation, he could look over the wall and see the whole length of the canyon. Puffs of smoke no longer drifted into the sky, but now there was other movement. Riders in the pines on the slopes of the canyon.

'You heard him!' Reverend Burt Roberts bellowed. 'Close the gates before the heathen get here!'

Dave Calhoun and Jed Bliss threw themselves against the heavy gates. As the two settlers heaved, the old gates dragged on the tufts of coarse grass which grew over the entrance. Finally, the barrier was in place. Roberts dropped the iron bar.

'Preacher,' Kozlov summoned him

from the platform. The settlers were all inside the stockade walls.

Bliss had arrived first with his Indian squaw trailing a few steps behind. It was the first-time Anton had seen her. She was a young Crow, slim and stately. Grayson Weathers, his young wife, Clara, and Calhoun had come next.

Weathers was standing protectively beside his pregnant wife. In his free hand, he held his rifle.

Calhoun was armed to the teeth. He wore a double gun rig and carried three rifles and a double-barreled shotgun. Will Alvord and Crazy Jane stood apart from the others. The old mountain man had a massive hunting rifle slung over his shoulder.

Reverend Roberts, Henrietta and the preacher's six children from his three marriages, had lumbered down the valley in a wagon pulled by a team of sweating horses. Anton had come in last.

'The gate's barred,' Roberts said.

Built like a shaggy bull, he was no seminary-trained preacher. He held church weekly in his barn where he preached earthy sermons, baptized babies and performed marriages and funerals. He looked more at home wielding an ax or a shovel than thumping a Bible. Anton rarely attended the preacher's services, but he liked the man.

'What is next, Kozlov?' the preacher was asking now.

Anton glanced back over the stockade. The army had built the outpost well. The four straight log walls made a precise square. They enclosed an old, dusty building, once used as store and barracks. In the center of the old parade ground was a stone-walled well which Will Alvord had already checked. The bucket he had lowered by rope came up full of fresh, cold, drinking water. Alongside the one-time barracks was a stable and a small guardhouse with barred windows. A two-story building, the former officers' quarters, was set into the eastern wall. Kozlov's eyes swept along the platform. There would be six settlers to man the four walls.

'Stable the horses and then pool the food,' Anton ordered the bearded preacher. 'The women can handle that, because I want every man on this platform with his guns loaded.'

'I will make sure it is done,' Burt Roberts promised, leaving him to watch the canyon.

Anton had assumed command the moment he rode into the stockade, and no one argued with him. He had been a cavalry scout, former Russian soldier; he knew Indians and the way they thought. Besides, he had won the respect of the Devil's Canyon folks a year before, when the Tully gang came to plunder. Single-handedly, he had put paid to Steven Tully and his two sidekicks. That was enough to send the rest of the outfit fleeing for their lives.

The timbered slopes were alive with riders now, descending into the canyon. This was no small raiding party. The Paiute Indians were swarming like bees. Even as he watched, settlers took up positions on the platform. Will Alvord and Jed Bliss were manning the western wall, Dave Calhoun and Grayson Weathers climbed the ladder on the south side.

The preacher rejoined him and asked, 'Are the red varmints still coming for us?'

Anton nodded. 'They are headed this way, for sure.'

'Smoke!' Roberts pointed out.

'It is not a signal, preacher,' Anton told him with his eyes on the black, swirling cloud. 'They have torched a cabin. I would say Will Alvord and Crazy Jane will be rebuildin'.'

'If they ... I mean ... we survive the attack,' the preacher added.

'Yes, exactly.'

'Heathen vandals!' Reverend Roberts cried passionately, keeping an anxious eye on the distant slope where his own cabin stood.

'There has to be a reason for this,' Anton murmured.

'They are all children of the devil,' Roberts pronounced. He glanced down at the weed-strewn parade ground and jerked his chin in the direction of Bliss' young squaw. 'And we have let one of them inside with us! I don't like it, Kozlov! If we are still here after dark, she could knife any of us in the back.'

'So could you … or I … or anyone one of us for that matter,' Anton replied. 'She belongs to a white man. That means she is tainted and a candidate for scalpin', same as us. No cause to worry about her.'

'They didn't worry about Judas either,' Roberts reminded him as he stared at her with obvious distaste. 'How could any Christian white man cohabit with an Indian squaw?'

'Preacher,' Anton said softly, 'I reckon they are at your place.'

Reverend Burt Roberts whipped his gaze from Bliss' squaw and looked north. His eyes were dark and wide and terrible as they fastened on the black pall belching into the sky. He clenched his huge fists and shook them at the smoke that rose.

'They will burn in hell for this!' Roberts promised, as fiery sparks mingled with the black smoke.

Two minutes later, a new plume of smoke began to rise, and Anton swore under his breath. Now it was his cabin. Anger and frustration swept over him as he watched the smoke thicken. The raiders were systematically burning every cabin in Devil's Canyon, as they moved towards the stockade.

From his elevated position, Anton Kozlov spotted a large bunch fording the river. He glanced anxiously up at the pass and hoped that Lucy was safe.

Maybe Judd had already led his bride and the troopers through the pass, and they were on their way to Fort Bighorn. For all his faults, Judd was a good cavalryman.

Anton turned his eyes down canyon again. A second bunch of warriors was fording the river, and smoke was rising from Dave Calhoun's new cabin.

'Keep watch,' Anton told the preacher. 'I will check right along the walls.'

Walking along the platform, he headed towards Calhoun. The loner stood staring over the eastern wall. He held the double-barreled shotgun in his arms, and his rifles rested beside him. Anton halted a few paces away, but Calhoun did not acknowledge his presence.

'We expect them within the hour,' Anton said gloomily.

Calhoun nodded. 'I will be ready.'

'Watch those rocks,' Anton warned. 'If there is an attack, they will want that spot, so they can keep blastin' this wall.'

Calhoun fixed his cold eyes on the jumbled rocks.

'No need to give me advice, Kozlov. When it comes to swappin' lead, I know what to do.' He spat over the wall. 'I reckon you would have heard about that.'

It was Anton's turn to nod. 'I have heard some talk.'

'I could use some tobacco,' Calhoun declared.

Kozlov handed his pouch to the tall, lean settler. Putting down his shotgun, Calhoun built himself a cigarette.

'I reckon they got your cabin,' Anton

said as Calhoun lit his cigarette.

'I can build another,' Calhoun simply replied.

Anton left him and walked along the south platform. This wall overlooked a lightly-timbered downslope. Seeing Kozlov approaching, Grayson Weathers lowered his rifle.

'You OK here, Grayson?' Anton asked.

'I'm OK,' Weathers said. 'I am just worried about Clara. She is due pretty shortly.'

Anton looked concerned. 'How soon, Grayson?'

The man shrugged. 'I dunno ... a couple of days maybe.'

'The other women will look after her,' Anton said to reassure him.

'Kozlov,' Weathers said slowly, 'if those red devils get in and kill all the men, what will happen to the women folk?'

'Never you mind that,' Anton replied softly, 'just keep your eyes on that slope, you hear?'

The man nodded. 'I am keeping my last bullet for Clara.'

'You do what you have to do,' Anton told him gently.

He left Weathers swigging water from his canteen. From the western wall, he saw more smoke. Just about every cabin in Devil's Canyon was blazing. He glanced down at the parade ground. The horses were all stabled. By now, most of the women were inside the two-story building, although he could see Bliss' young squaw seated cross-legged in the dust

'Any bright ideas?' Will Alvord asked.

'All I know is we are not goin' to lay down and die,' Anton told him. 'We have food, water in the well, and ammunition.'

'Listen, Kozlov, you damn well know we don't have enough guns or ammunition to hold off that many Indians,' Bliss said wryly.

With a slight nod of his head and looking down then up again, Anton said, 'We are goin' to try.'

A sudden burst of gunfire made Bliss and Alvord grab their rifles. It was distant gunfire coming from the direction of the pass, and the echoes rolled and merged like faraway thunder. The echoes died, and then there was more gunfire. A lone smoke signal puffed above the pass. It was a signal summoning more warriors in for the kill.

'You said that the lieutenant's outfit and a woman tried to make it?' Alvord recalled. 'Looks like they are in trouble. Big trouble. Even Preacher Roberts' prayers could not save them now.'

Anton Kozlov stared helplessly at the pass. The gunfire faded. Stillness gripped Devil's Canyon once more.

The stillness stretched to nearly five minutes.

Anton imagined the wicked flash of scalping knives, and he felt sick in the pit of his stomach as he thought about Lesya — Lucy's possible fate. He smoked a cigarette. Then another. Finally, he returned to Reverend Roberts on the north wall.

Six separate palls of smoke hung over the canyon.

The Paiute Indians had crossed the

river. The main bunch would be threading through a pine forest, coming closer to the stockade. Anton glanced at the pass. The smoke puffs were no longer rising but he could detect a thin veneer of dust masking the sun.

'I will check that the women are OK,' Anton decided.

'Look!' the preacher said urgently. 'Look west — riders approaching!'

Branches were swaying as blue-coated riders emerged cautiously from the trees. Anton counted five soldiers, glimpsed Lucy Doniphon riding behind the others. They drew rein and surveyed the boulder-strewn grass which sloped down to the stockade wall. Anton recognized the lead rider as Lieutenant Judd Reed. Right at that moment, Kozlov caught a glimpse of more movement. About ten painted Paiute braves were riding out of the pines below the preacher's wall. Obviously, they were about to ride slap into the advance party riding against the stockade.

'Cover them, quick!' Anton said

tersely, raising his rifle.

Two rifles boomed together. Anton's first bullet smashed into a Paiute Indian's chest and lifted him clean out of the saddle. The preacher's slug burned into a young buck's shoulder. Yelling with rage, the scouts reached for weapons as Judd and his troopers charged desperately towards the outpost.

'Open the gate!' Anton yelled.

Jed Bliss' squaw and Crazy Jane ran towards the entrance. Anton's Hawken rifle thundered twice in rapid succession, and two more Paiute warriors slumped against their horses' necks like wet sacks. An older Paiute Indian with long, gray braids, aimed his army carbine at the incoming riders, but Reverend Roberts cut him down with one careful shot. An arrow thudded into the stockade wall just below Kozlov. The troopers were firing now, and a barrage of flying lead lashed the exposed Indians. Ponies reared. Two braves toppled to the ground. One clawed his way back to his feet, but Hal Yacey shot him dead. The three remaining Indian braves wheeled their ponies and set them galloping back to cover. The two women at the gate lifted the iron bar. Judd and his troopers thundered down from the ridge, weaving between boulders and racing through the grass. One of the marauders had stayed hidden behind a boulder. Now he reared up with a rifle aimed straight at Judd Reed. Trooper Ben Copeland fired a single shot and the warrior fell back among the boulders.

Judd was the first rider through the gate. He hustled into the outpost in a cloud of swirling dust. Next came Trooper Yacey, brandishing his rifle. Copeland and Tuck Gravens squeezed through the entrance together. Finally, Lucy Doniphon rode alongside Trooper Alan Loomis. The young soldier had blood on his tunic, and he sagged in the saddle. The gate had been opened just wide enough to allow two horses through at once, and now Crazy Jane's husband shouldered it shut. Jane and Jed Bliss' squaw lifted the iron bar back over the hooks of the gate.

Anton climbed down the ladder on the platform.

The riders were plastered with dust. Lieutenant Reed was trying to control his prancing horse. He had a smear of blood down his right cheek, his eye was black and swollen, and his tunic was also stained with blood. Yacey and Gravens dismounted as the lieutenant finally calmed his horse and looked around the parade ground inside the stockade. Approaching the blue-coated troopers, Anton heard Loomis groan.

'Murdering bastards!' Judd raged as the mountain man glanced around the walls to make sure they were all manned.

'We — we rode straight into an ambush,' Trooper Loomis whispered.

'We almost made it,' Judd told his former stepfather, 'but when we couldn't fight our way through, we had to retreat back before a bigger bunch could get to us … ' He slipped his rifle back into its sheath. 'So here we are. This seemed to be the only sensible place to go.'

'I will help you down, Lucy,' Anton offered.

'Thank you, Anton,' she said faintly.

Judd remained in his saddle. His bride-to-be placed her hands on Anton's broad shoulders, and her fingers lingered on his muscular strength as he lifted her down.

'The women are in there,' Anton said, indicating the tall building. 'You had best join them, Lucy. You might take a look at Mrs Weathers, too. She is expectin'.'

'Certainly,' she said, stepping away from him.

'You stop a slug, trooper?' Anton asked Trooper Loomis.

'He is just winged,' Judd spoke for him.

'We don't have a real doctor here, but the preacher can likely take care of this,' Anton told the young man. 'I will fetch him down.'

Alan Loomis winced and more blood welled through his tunic.

'I – I will be OK … '

'Reverend!' Anton called, 'we need you

142

down here pronto!' He looked straight at Gravens as he said, 'Soldier, you can relieve the preacher at his post.'

Judd Reed's frown darkened.

'Old Moscow ... Anton ... these are my men. I will give the orders to them. In fact, since we are here, I am assuming full authority over this stockade.'

'Soldier,' the mountain man repeated, 'relieve the preacher.'

'Now, listen here — ' the lieutenant snarled.

'Kozlov!' Reverend Roberts' voice thundered over the outpost. 'Anton Kozlov, come up here — now!'

Anton wasted little time as he loped across the parade ground to the foot of the ladder. By the time he climbed the rungs, attackers were pouring out of the pine forest in a wave of painted men and daubed ponies.

Anton and the others had not slept much the night before, for they stayed awake watching the ridges and prepared to take a shot at the attacking Paiutes that tried to storm the stockade. Anton, like the others, was tired, sleeping little of late so he was awfully tired when he climbed the ladder to the platform.

Revered Roberts' face was chalk-white, and his quivering lips framed a fervent, mumbled prayer. He clutched the top of the stockade stakes. Still the warriors came, flooding through the trees on to the flats in front of the outpost.

Anton watched them. Near-naked, they were painted for war. Bronze and decked with feathers, they rode shaggy, paint-daubed ponies. Some carried guns, but more brandished tomahawks and long lances, There were no war cries. In fact, everything was happening in an uncanny silence.

The Paiute chief, Iron Crow, was there himself — a straight-backed veteran on a creamy-white stallion.

Anton recognized two of the old man's sons, haughty Bear Heart and the crafty Blue Falcon. He saw the medicine man, Wind Shawl, and two lesser chiefs, Yellow Hawk and Ancient Fire. A little apart from the others was Kills Many, the renegade. This was the first time Kills Many had been seen by a white man for some years.

Anton heard the tramp of boots beside him.

'Judas Priest!' Lieutenant Judd Reed croaked as he came up beside his stepfather.

'They are starting to circle us,' Reverend Burt Roberts said hoarsely.

Lines of mounted warriors rode away from the main bunch to form a circle around the outpost. They rode slowly and deliberately as if contemptuous of the defenders' guns. Troopers Yacey and Gravens were beside their lieutenant now, and their eyes were wide with something very much like fear.

'Reverend, there is a wounded soldier down on the parade ground,' Anton informed Roberts.

'I will take a look at him,' Roberts said, apparently grateful for a reason to take his eyes away from the circling Paiute Indians.

Tuck Gravens took the preacher's place. There was no argument now from the lieutenant. He seemed hypnotized by the spectacle beyond the walls.

'Know something?' Judd said finally. 'That butcher, Iron Crow, is just about in rifle range. I could pick the bastard off here and now! I have heard about these Snake Indians! The moment their chief dies, they go into mourning. They hold a funeral service which lasts for days on end. They even lay down their weapons — '

'You have been readin' too many dime novels about Apaches, Comanches, and other tribes,' Anton said. 'Don't do what you just said.'

'So, what is your suggestion then, Old Moscow?' Judd asked sneeringly.

'We wait and see what happens.'

The circle was complete. The Paiute warriors simply sat their ponies, watching the stockade walls. A couple of braves built a fire. One by one, the chiefs sat down.

'What in tarnation is going on?' Gra-

146

vens demanded.

'They are havin' a pow-wow,' Anton observed. 'They won't attack today, so relax and check your hardware.'

'Relax?' Gravens squeaked. 'How the hell can we relax with those goddamn savages surrounding us?'

Leaving Judd and Trooper Gravens on the platform, Anton returned to the parade ground. He went to the two-story house and opened the door. The women had dropped their belongings along one wall, and food was stockpiled in the middle of the long room. Crazy Jane and Clara Weathers were helping the preacher's wife with her brood of six children. Jed Bliss' squaw had lit the stove. They had made a makeshift bed out of an old mattress, and Lucy was assisting Reverend Roberts as he bent over the young soldier.

'How is he doin'?' Anton wanted to know.

'He will need some whiskey because it is sure gonna hurt when I dig out the bullet.'

'It is right against the bone,' Lucy told him.

Her eyes met Anton's over the bed.

'The reverend says there are splinters of bone that have to come out,' she added.

'Quite a few, in fact,' the preacher said. He glanced at Bliss' squaw. 'Hurry up with that fire, woman. I want to heat my knife blade.'

'My name is Flat Face Chante,' the squaw stated.

'Make it fast, Flat Face,' Burt Roberts repeated.

Crazy Jane joined them.

'Did I hear you say you wanted whiskey?' she asked.

'It is the devil's brew, but this man will need some for the pain,' Roberts confirmed.

'My man packed some away,' Jane said. 'I will find you a bottle.'

The bottle was fetched and the knife sterilized. Lucy lifted the bottle to Trooper Loomis' lips. With the preacher advising him to drink every last drop of the strong-smelling brew, Alan Loomis began to swallow obediently. When he was glassy-eyed, he flopped back on the mattress.

'Hold him down now,' Robert said simply.

The preacher jammed a piece of wood between Loomis' lips and started to slice into the wound. He was quick and decisive. Trooper Loomis' eyes bulged in terrible agony, but Lucy and Crazy Jane held him to the mattress. The knife delved further, and Roberts produced a long splinter of bone. Next, he drew out a bullet between his thumb and forefinger.

'Kozlov!' Trooper Copeland called from the doorway. 'The lieutenant wants you on the north wall. There is an Indian riding towards the gate!'

Anton ran across the parade ground and up the ladder. The chiefs and elders were now standing and watching as the Paiute Indian, Yellow Hawk, rode his pony slowly towards the stockade gate. He carried a lance. Tied to its point was a piece of white cloth which fluttered in the morning breeze.

6

An Indian's Justice

'A flag of truce?' Judd Reed sneered. 'It has to be some kind of trick!'

The Paiute Indian rode closer. He was an old man, probably too old to fight. He wore a faded, yellow hat over his graying hair. His doeskin shirt gaped at the neck, betraying a bony, wrinkled chest. Yellow Hawk kept riding, only drawing rein in the very shadow of the stockade wall.

'Open the gate,' Anton said.

'Like hell we will,' Judd exploded.

'Iron Crow will honor his white flag,' Anton insisted. 'I am goin' out to speak with him.'

'You are damn crazy!' Trooper Hal Yacey joined in. 'Once those gates are open, we will all be done for.'

'The man wants to talk,' Anton said patiently. 'That is a whole lot better than fightin'.'

Anton signaled to Bliss, who ran across the parade ground. While the settler lifted the bar and pulled open the gate, Anton untied his gun-belt, and rested his rifle against the stockade wall. Women came out of the two-story building, tentatively. Lucy ran forward before Anton could walk outside.

'Be careful,' she whispered.

'How is the soldier boy doin'?' Anton asked in reply.

'Reverend Roberts says he will be all right.' She grasped his arm and said, 'I will be praying for you.'

'You do that, Lucy.'

He stepped outside and heard the gate close behind him as he started towards Yellow Hawk, The Paiute Indians watched him unblinkingly as he advanced.

'I speak the Paiute tongue if that will please you,' Anton Kozlov said.

'That is good,' Yellow Hawk said, 'and we know you speak that tongue. Looks at the Bear is with us. You remember him, white man?'

Anton nodded. 'I remember him.'

'You spared his life,' Yellow Hawk stated. 'It is because of this that Iron Crow has decided to talk and to give you a chance to save many lives.'

With a look of complete seriousness, Anton replied, 'I am ready to listen.'

'Follow me, white man.'

Yellow Hawk turned his pony's head and started slowly towards the council fire. Anton walked behind him, leaving the stockade shadow. He came closer to the mounted warriors and saw the hatred on their faces. Anton kept walking. Finally, Yellow Hawk nudged his pony into a lope, leaving the white man standing beside the council fire. Iron Crow stepped forward. Beside him, the renegade Kills Many, glared at the frontiersman. The medicine man, Wind Shawl, kept his distance.

Despite his age, Iron Crow was still a towering figure of a man. His face was craggy and lined. His nose looked like it had been broken many years ago. His lips were thin and bloodless, but his ancient

153

eyes were alive and alert.

'It is I who sent the white flag,' he said. 'We will talk, and then you will return unharmed.'

'I told those inside the stockade the truth when I said you were a man of honor,' Anton said.

'We will sit down,' Chief Iron Crow told him.

The Paiute Indian chief folded like a jackknife and sat in the dust warmed by the glowing embers of the fire. Anton squatted down beside him.

'You are on the warpath for reasons I do not know,' Anton Kozlov said slowly. 'You have the men and weapons to kill and scalp us all.'

'This is so.'

'Yet you choose to talk?'

'Yellow Hawk gave you the reason.'

'Because I spared the life of an old man who raided my traps?' Anton asked.

'You spared his life and saved him from the blue-coats soldiers who would have killed him.' The chief paused. 'Looks at the Bear is my blood brother.'

Iron Crow's words hung in the silence between them. It was a silence broken by a crackle of wood in the council fire. Behind the chief, Wind Shawl hovered with folded arms. His harsh face was a mask of unrelenting hatred.

'A crime has been committed against our people,' the old medicine man announced. His tone had turned cold and bitter. 'It was a crime so shameful that my people have sought revenge in blood. White settlers in wagons have been attacked and scalped. My braves have burned homes and spilled much blood.'

'There is a treaty, Wind Shawl,' Anton reminded him.

The medicine man raised his knife and spat into the dust inches from Anton's boots.

'White men broke the treaty!' Iron Crow said passionately.

'What did these white men do?'

'My granddaughter was with the other young women from the village,' Iron Crow said heavily. 'She was purifying herself before her wedding.' The old man's lips made a thin, tight line. 'White riders came. They took the maidens by force, and then — they killed them all.'

'Iron Crow, I am sorry,' Anton said.

'My scouts found the trail,' Iron Crow declared. 'The trail led here — to this valley.' The chief's eyes were expressionless. 'The white dogs who raped and murdered the maidens are inside your walls, Kozlov!'

'You are sure of this?'

'Yes. Kozlov, I am offering to spare your life and the lives of everyone under your protection — except the evil ones.'

'Who are these killers?' Anton asked.

'The soldiers,' Iron Crow hissed. He raised his right hand and added, 'Five murderers.'

Anton Kozlov stared at him.

There had to be some mistake. Maybe the scouts had latched on to the wrong trail. But Anton remembered Old Bootleg Canyon. He knew what some blue-coats, including his own stepson, were capable of doing.

'Your head knows it is true, but your heart does not want to believe,' the Indian said perceptively. 'I will show you something.' He called to his medicine man, and a Paiute called Last Buffalo came forward with a shred of fabric. It was ragged, ripped and blue. It was unmistakably a piece of torn tunic. 'Kozlov, I found this in the hand of my granddaughter.'

Last Buffalo shoved the dirty, blue rag into Anton's hand. Revulsion and anger swept over him.

'I would like to keep this,' Anton said after a long silence.

'When you return to the stockade you will find one of the white dogs has his tunic torn,' the Paiute chief predicted. 'That piece you hold will fit the tear.'

'These men should be brought to justice,' Anton said. 'They must face a military court and be punished.'

Iron Crow shook his head.

'We are not fools, Kozlov! We do not trust soldier justice! You will give the criminals to us, and they will all die in a way the council decides.'

'Listen, chief — '

'You were brought here to listen to me, Kozlov, and I have spoken,' Iron Crow interrupted. 'Send out the soldiers who have blood on their hands, and I will spare the others.' The old chief rose to his feet, signifying that the interview was at the end. 'You have until the sun is at its highest, Kozlov. If the soldiers are not put outside the gates before then, everyone in that outpost will die. Hear my words, Kozlov. Blood will run like a river!'

'I will think on your words, Iron Crow.'

'Go, Kozlov,' the chief said in dismissal. 'You walk safely back to the stockade.'

Iron Crow folded his arms. Standing a shadow's length away, the medicine man, Last Buffalo, stared like a snake about to strike. Anton walked past the shaman and set his face for the outpost. A drum sounded. Paiute Indians brandished weapons as the white man headed across the open ground. He did not look back.

158

He just walked slowly, taking his time. It would have been of no use to argue with Iron Crow. The chief had given him a straightforward choice: hand over the five soldiers to pay for their crime or everyone inside the outpost, including the innocent, would be butchered.

Kozlov knew full well what penalties the guilty men would face. A slow-roasting over the torture fires was the most likely ending for Judd and the four troopers if they were surrendered to the Paiute Indians. Worse still, they could be given to the squaws. No death was slower and more agonizing than their razor-sharp skinning knives. Anton could not see himself surrendering anyone to such a death, let alone someone who was his stepson. The alternative was even more terrible, however — violent death for everyone in the stockade, guilty and innocent alike. He thought of Lucy Doniphon, starting a new life — Clara Weathers heavy with child — young Trooper Loomis.

He kept walking.

The ring of warriors was like a pack

of hunting dogs waiting to be unleashed. Anton was under no illusions. There was simply not enough firepower in the stockade. They might withstand two charges with luck on their side, but sheer weight of numbers would swamp the defenders then. Once the walls were scaled, the butchery would begin.

No one would be spared in the blood-letting frenzy. Damn the lieutenant! Damn the soldiers who had betrayed their uniforms!

The drumming was mounting to a wild crescendo as he walked into the shadow of the stockade wall.

He headed straight for the gate. Judd's sharp command rang out and Anton heard the scrape of the heavy, iron bar. Big hands pulled the gate open just a little, and Anton stepped through the gap. Trooper Hal Yacey kicked the gate shut.

'Well?' Judd demanded from the platform above. 'You were out there long enough with those savages.'

Anton looked around the stockade. The settlers were all at their posts. Tuck

Gravens stood beside his lieutenant. Ben Copeland smoked a cigar while pacing the western platform. Yacey replaced the iron bar back on the gate. Lucy stood anxiously in the doorway of the officers' quarters. Anton picked up his rifle and gun belt.

'I want everyone out here,' Kozlov announced. 'There is somethin' everyone needs to hear.'

Judd's eyes narrowed as he asked, 'What is it?'

'You can hear it right along with everybody else,' Anton said tersely.

'Yacey,' he said to the nearest trooper, 'spread the word.'

'And leave all the walls unguarded?' Hal Yacey asked incredulously.

'We are safe till noon,' Anton reassured.

Yacey looked to his lieutenant for advice.

'Lieutenant?' he queried.

'Do what he says,' Judd Reed told the frowning trooper.

Anton turned and started across the

parade ground. As he waited near the women's shelter, he rolled a cigarette. Lucy came to stand beside her future husband. Clara stepped awkwardly into the square, followed by the other women. The preacher's wife lingered in the open doorway, keeping an eye on her patient, Trooper Loomis. Anton lit his cigarette as the men approached. He drew deeply until everyone was near enough to hear him.

'I have spoken with Iron Crow, the chief,' he began. 'I believe him to be an honorable man, and he has offered us a deal.' He flicked his cigarette and looked around the circle of soldiers and settlers. 'Iron Crow told me that five soldiers violated and murdered some Paiute maidens.' As he paused, Yacey's hand moved to his holster. Copeland and Gravens exchanged glances. Lieutenant Judd Reed's face turned ashen. 'The chief said their trail led here.'

'You mean — to this stockade?' Reverend Roberts asked hoarsely.

'Chief Iron Crow said the blue-coats are in here right now,' Anton said simply. 'His deal is this. If those soldiers are handed over to his warriors for punishment, there will be no more killin'.'

'And if we do not?' Jed Bliss asked.

'They will kill us all and probably stay on the warpath after that,' Anton replied.

'So, what did you tell the stinking Injun?' Judd demanded.

Anton did not answer him.

'I want to show you somethin',' he said soberly. He reached into his hip pocket and took out the ragged piece of blue tunic. Then he held the shred of material high to the wind until it fluttered. 'Anyone recognize this?'

'What is that supposed to mean?' Trooper Ben Copeland sneered.

'Don't waste our time, Kozlov!' Tuck Gravens warned.

'I notice a tear in the back of your tunic, Judd,' Anton said. 'I reckon this piece fits it real snug.'

Judd's face darkened, and the muscle just below his swollen left eye started to twitch, as much as it could as battered as it was. He rested his right hand on his holstered army pistol.

'What the hell are you getting at, Old Moscow?' Judd demanded in a voice heavy with menace.

'This piece of army tunic was found in the hand of one of the dead women,' Anton said. 'She had been raped and her throat had been cut.'

'And you believe the word of a dirty, stinking Injun?' Judd exploded scornfully.

Anton eyed the officer. 'I am goin' to ask you straight.'

'Ask away,' Judd Reed challenged.

'Did you and your troopers do it or not? Somebody in a US army uniform killed those women ... '

There was a long, painful silence. Lucy Doniphon's hand fell from Judd's arm, and she stepped away from him without looking at him.

'You bastard!' Judd hissed.

Hal Yacey had his Colt halfway out of the holster.

'Just say the word, Lieutenant, and I will …'

'No, you won't soldier!' Reverend Burt Roberts roared behind his leveled rifle. 'Put that hardware back where it belongs, or as God is my judge, I will send you to hell right this very minute!' The preacher waited until Yacey dropped the pistol back into its leather. 'That's better. Now I want to hear some answers to Anton's question.'

'I – I will give you an answer,' Trooper Alan Loomis cried from inside the building where he lay.

'Button your goddamn lip, Loomis!' Judd snapped harshly.

'You are sick, Loomis; go rest up,' Yacey advised him.

'Yes, 1 am sick, all right, but I am not the only one,' Trooper Loomis called back. 'We were all sick that afternoon. You, me, the lieutenant — all of us …'

'Shut his mouth!' Judd snarled.

Roberts backed to the door, his rifle leveled.

'We are going to hear Trooper Loomis,'

he said sternly.

'Sorry, Lieutenant,' Loomis apologized, 'but these folks dug out my bullet and tended to me. Since their lives are at stake, the least I owe them is the truth!'

'We are listenin', Loomis,' Anton said.

'Loomis, I will tell them what happened!' Judd cut in. 'I am in command here, and it is my place to speak.' He folded his arms and eyed the settlers. 'Listen to me and judge for yourselves. We were riding back after doing our sworn duty, which happened to be tracking down some yellow deserters who didn't have the decency to stand up for their own kind … We came across some squaws. There they were, cavorting around without a stitch of clothing on. For anybody that doesn't know already, they are not like our white women. You could have any of them for a plug of tobacco.' He grinned and winked at the valley men. 'Well, we did what comes naturally — we just helped ourselves.'

'It is what they expected,' Copeland chimed in.

'Useless Injun trash,' Yacey added. 'I don't know what the hell all the fuss is about!'

'Hal's right,' Judd said.

Lucy took another step away from the soldier she had promised to marry.

'Judd,' she said in the heavy silence. 'I came all this way to be your wife. Why couldn't you wait for me? Why did you have to do this?'

The lieutenant turned on her savagely: 'Shut your mouth, woman! I am a man!'

'Don't worry, ma'am,' Yacey laughed. 'They weren't white women, just Injuns. Trash. It didn't mean a thing, and it don't count for nothing.'

'That is not quite right,' Anton said solemnly. 'The young woman Judd attacked was Chief Iron Crow's granddaughter. He raped and killed a princess.'

'Crap!' Judd hissed.

'You raped her, and then you slit her throat,' Anton accused.

'It was their fault,' Hal Yacey mumbled. 'One of them pulled a knife. What were we supposed to do?'

'Like Hal said, they were all Injun trash anyway,' Judd shrugged.

'Trash? It is clear to see who the real trash is,' Anton said slowly, visibly upset.

Judd Reed bristled with anger.

'Quit your goddamn preaching, you Injun-lover!'

'I seem to remember that is what you said at Old Bootleg Canyon, too.' Kozlov reminded him. 'You raped and killed helpless Indians then. You have not changed at all.'

'Forget about Old Bootleg Canyon,' Judd advised him darkly.

'Forget about it? How could anyone forget about that?' Anton demanded. 'You led a charge into the village. Lice like Yacey here rode with you, smokin' cigars and laughin' like it was a wild turkey shoot. You raped the young women, and you shot anyone who moved — old men, women, even children.'

'The court martial didn't see it that way,' Lieutenant Judd Reed smirked. 'Remember? They weren't about to believe the evidence of a quitter who

168

would go against his own family.'

'We are family,' Anton shot back. He walked towards the lieutenant, halting directly in front of him.

'I will give you a history lesson, Judd,' he said. 'I admitted to bein' dazed at the time. That was because I protested when you gave the order, and one of your troopers smashed a rifle into the back of my head so I couldn't spoil your fun. I was dazed, Judd, but I saw and heard enough.'

'Whatever the reason, we were acquitted,' the lieutenant insisted. 'No military court convicts a soldier for killing savages — not then, not now. Killing savages like these Paiutes ain't a crime.'

'Iron Crow doesn't see it like that, and he is holdin' all the high cards this time,' Anton reminded him.

'So, what are you gonna do, Old Moscow?' Judd jeered. 'Try to turn us over to those heathen savages to save your own skin?'

Gravens and Copeland lifted their rifles and stepped back. Forming a line of three, Trooper Hal Yacey wrapped his fingers around his holstered gun. Their lieutenant joined them, and the four uniformed men stood there defiantly, daring anyone to make a move. Anton glanced at the settlers. Weathers and Bliss just gaped, baffled and nervous. No one had seen Dave Calhoun draw his gun but the .45 was in his hands and leveled. Beside him, Will Alvord had his double-barreled shotgun aimed at the blue-coats and his thick fingers were already curled around the triggers. Reverend Roberts' eyes blazed with righteous fury.

'There are innocent women and children, not to mention an unborn babe, in this stockade,' Roberts thundered. 'If you had any decency, anything remotely resembling a conscience, you and your troopers would walk out there and take what is coming to you.'

'Save the sermon, preacher,' Judd scoffed. 'There is no chance of us doing that, and no one here has the guts to try to make us!'

'Don't push your luck,' Calhoun said

coldly.

'That is good advice,' Will Alvord said flatly.

Anton stood between the blue-coats and the angry settlers.

'Swappin' lead won't solve anythin'. When I put the cards on the table, I was givin' these men a chance to do what is right. I am not surprised that they turned out to be yellow.

'These gutless excuses for cavalrymen will have to live with their cowardice. We don't have the right to force any man to walk out to a torture fire.' Anton appraised them all. 'We have no choice now but to stand together.'

7

Traitors and Hell-Fire

The drums had stopped — all thought thankfully and nervously.

What did it mean?

There was a long silence broken only by the sound of the wind. Hardly a shadow darkened Devil's Canyon. Within minutes the sun would be at its zenith.

Anton Kozlov's eyes swept over the last outpost west — the stockade. Men with rifles watched and waited.

Dave Calhoun had resumed his position at the eastern wall. He was one who had disagreed with Anton. He would have taken his chances against Judd and his troopers and handed over any blue-coat survivors to the Paiute Indians. Maybe Calhoun was right.

Right now, Trooper Tuck Gravens was joining him on the eastern platform. Grayson Weathers and Will

Alvord manned the south wall with Alan Loomis. They had hauled the wounded trooper to his feet and helped him to the platform where he stood propped up against the wall. Jed Bliss, Burt Roberts and Trooper Ben Copeland lined the western extremities of the stockade. Judd Reed and Trooper Hal Yacey stood together on the parade ground. Except for Lucy Doniphon, the women were inside, huddled together upstairs where the officers used to sleep when the stockade had been active.

Suddenly the drums sounded again, and the Paiute Indians began to chant. The painted warriors moved their ponies a few paces closer, just like a noose being tightened. Yellow Hawk and Wind Shawl broke through the circle and sat staring at the stockade walls.

'Anton, what are they doing?' Lucy asked as she approached the older mountain man.

'It is the death chant,' he told her coldly.

Lucy looked around the painted circle

of Indian warriors.

'We are all going to die, aren't we?' she asked dully.

'It doesn't look good for us, Lucy,' the mountain man admitted.

She clasped his left arm, clinging to him.

'We rode together for a long time. You could have told me what kind of man the lieutenant was.'

'At the time, I had my reasons for not sayin' anythin' about him,' Anton said.

'Oh, OK.'

He looked straight at her. She was so close he could have wrapped his right arm around her. Their eyes met and held as the awesome death chant from the Paiute rose to a terrible crescendo.

'Like I said, I had my reasons, Lucy,' Anton said as the chanting ended abruptly. 'But things have changed. I am goin' to tell you why I said nothin'. We rode, we shared grub, we faced danger together. And although you were the lieutenant's intended bride, I began to want you for myself, as you remind me of my late wife, Lesya.' He felt her fingers dig into his arm like she never wanted to let him go. 'I knew I was too old for you and that not tellin' you wasn't right...'

'Anton — ' she cut him short hoarsely.

'Yes?'

'I want you to know something.' She swallowed hard. 'Anton, from the moment we met, I wished you were the man I had come west to marry! Despite our age difference.'

The shaman, Wind Shawl, slid from his pony. Clutching a long lance, he advanced half a dozen paces and thrust the spear point into the dusty clay. It cast a tiny, shrinking shadow, no longer than a man's finger. When that shadow was no more, the Paiute would come.

Anton heard the thud of boots on the wooden platform. Turning sharply, he glimpsed Trooper Gravens well away from his post. Anton's angry eyes swept around the stockade platform. Both the eastern and western walkways were empty. Down on the parade ground, Calhoun was heading for the officer's house.

Anton stared in amazement. He could not see Judd anywhere. In fact, the only blue-coat in sight was Trooper Gravens.

'Gravens!' Anton yelled furiously as Grayson Weathers descended the southern ladder. 'Gravens! What the hell is going on, damn you?'

'Lieutenant's orders!' Gravens bellowed back.

'The lieutenant's not in command!' Anton Kozlov roared angrily.

'Keep your shirt on, Kozlov,' Tuck Gravens called back. 'The lieutenant has some spare ammunition. He gave me orders to send every settler to the house to collect. You are included, Kozlov.'

'That damn fool order has left the walls unmanned,' noted Anton.

'It is ten minutes to noon,' Gravens argued, consulting his fob watch. The watch was a pocket watch attached to a chain. The fob or protective flap over the face and crystal of the watch was made of leather.

'We might as well have that spare ammunition, Anton,' Will Alvord hollered, tumbling down the ladder to join Weathers. 'We are gonna need every last bullet.'

Trooper Gravens turned the far corner and strode along the eastern wall towards Anton and Lucy. Big boots thumped the wooden boards. Anton returned his eyes to the painted warriors outside the stockade. Every Paiute Indian eye was on the lance's fading, diminishing shadow.

'You will need that ammunition, too,' Yacey said.

'Lucy,' Anton said tersely, 'please come with me.'

Anton was seething with anger. Maybe Judd had the best of intentions, but why didn't he send one of the troopers around the platforms with the extra ammunition? He sprang down the last few ladder rungs, reached up and helped Lucy to the ground.

He wanted to confront his former stepson, but this was not the place and there was certainly no time anyway. In fact, they barely had time to collect their shells and resume posts. Now Dave

Calhoun was inside, and Will Alvord was loping ahead of Grayson Weathers as they passed Reverend Burt Roberts' wagon. The two settlers barged through the door as Anton and Lucy started across the parade ground.

Drums once again began throbbing as Anton strode past the well.

There was hardly a shadow in the stockade. The sun was almost directly overhead. A lone vulture circled the outpost like a messenger of death.

Anton booted the door wide and walked straight into the naked muzzle of Trooper Hal Yacey's rifle.

'Don't move, Old Moscow,' Judd Reed warned, 'or Yacey here will blow your guts all over the floor.'

With Yacey's rifle point jammed against his belly, Anton froze in the doorway.

He heard Lucy Doniphon's startled gasp right behind him.

All five settlers were lined up against the far wall with their hands raised above their heads. Their holsters were empty, and their hardware heaped on the floor.

Judd and Trooper Ben Copeland were covering the settlers while Loomis stood unsteadily in the center of the room. The wounded trooper clutched a rifle in his shaking hands.

'It was a damnable lie!' Reverend Burt Roberts fumed. 'There is no spare ammunition! Like trusting sheep, we came inside one by one, so they could disarm us, Anton … '

'What is goin' on, Judd?' Anton demanded in cold fury. 'This is no time for games. The Paiute warriors are about to — '

'Only if they don't get what they want,' the army cavalry officer grinned.

'Walk!' Hal Yacey snarled. The trooper stepped to one side, his rifle still aimed at Anton's belly. 'Join your sodbuster friends, Old Moscow.'

'Do as you are told, Anton!' Judd snarled.

Slowly, Anton Kozlov started to walk towards the line of settlers.

'Anton!' Lucy screamed behind him. 'Look out — '

Anton threw himself sideways, but Yacey's rifle butt smashed into his neck. He crashed heavily to the floor. Dazed but still conscious, he groped for his gun and cleared leather. His head spun as Hal Yacey's bulky frame loomed over him. The rifle butt came down hard again, and darkness engulfed him like a black, evil tide.

'Woman, trying to warn my stepfather that way was a damn stupid thing to do,' Judd Reed grated. 'Don't you ever cross me again, old-timer!'

Lucy did not budge. Wet-eyed and trembling, she simply stared at the unconscious figure sprawled on the dusty floor. When she looked up at the man she had come so far to marry, there was hatred in her eyes.

'Move, ma'am,' Trooper Hal Yacey prodded.

'And close your eyes,' the lieutenant advised her. 'These settlers are about to strip naked.'

The five settlers stared at the lieutenant in absolute bewilderment.

'What kind of abomination is this?' Reverend Burt Roberts' voice boomed.

'You heard the lieutenant — take your clothes off,' Trooper Ben Copeland commanded sternly.

'Strip down! All of you! Pronto!' Yacey echoed harshly.

'NOW!' Judd Reed rasped, pointing his rifle at the preacher's head.

Cursing and muttering, the five unwilling settlers unbuttoned their shirts reluctantly. Hesitantly, they then began to unbuckle their belts. They attempted to delay the process as much as they could by moving slowly.

'Lieutenant, I don't like this — I don't like this one bit, sir,' young Trooper Alan Loomis protested strongly.

'You shut your trap,' Judd told the wounded cavalryman, 'and keep your gun trained on these settlers.'

Finally, five — all but one wore white, the Reverend wore a more traditional red union suit — all were complete with button placket fronts, button rear 'fireman's flap' with thick wrist and ankle cuffs — embarrassed men in faded long underwear stood facing the soldiers.

'Lieutenant Reed, I demand an explanation!' Reverend Burt Roberts roared.

'Be patient, Reverend,' Judd said mockingly. 'Isn't that what the Good Book teaches us?' He ran a critical eye along the row of half-dressed settlers. 'What do you reckon, Hal? Will we fit them all?' Yacey surveyed the burly preacher and said, 'The reverend is built like a damn buffalo, but I figure he will just squeeze into mine.'

'This is crazy talk —' Jed Bliss stormed.

'Gentlemen,' Judd announced with an icy grin plastered on his face, 'you are all gonna join the cavalry. I will cover you while you shuck off,' Judd said, turning to address his troopers then.

'You must be the lowest snakes ever to crawl out of hell,' the Reverend Roberts croaked as Trooper Tuck Gravens sauntered inside and unbuttoned his blue tunic.

'So, you have cottoned on, have you?' Lieutenant Judd Reed smirked. 'Congratulations! Chief Iron Crow wants some cavalrymen. Well, we are going to give him what he asked for.'

'You lousy bastards!' Grayson Weathers cried hoarsely.

'Think of it this way — you are being sacrificed so your womenfolk can live,' Yacey grinned.

'And rest assured, we will be looking after your women,' Ben Copeland chuckled merrily.

'May God forgive you, because we won't!' Reverend Roberts whispered.

'It is a military decision,' Judd shrugged. 'And the decision has been made.'

'Damn you all to hell!' Preacher Roberts thundered.

'Time for talk's over now, Preacher,' Judd snapped angrily. 'Get into those uniforms, pronto! And troopers, you keep your guns trained on them while I change my clothes.'

Crying silently, Lucy stood with her back to the wall. Upstairs, she heard the children crying as well.

'What about him?' Hal Yacey asked, pointing to Anton Kozlov's sprawled body.

'When they built this place, they dug out the cellar,' Judd recalled. 'There is a trapdoor in the corner. I will dump him down there and bolt it shut. There is no other way out.'

'Why don't. I just slit his throat and be done with it?' Yacey suggested coldly.

Judd Reed hesitated. 'He is a fool, but he did love my mother once, goddamn deserves better than that. The rats can take care of him, I reckon.'

'And just like that, you can wash your hands free of him?' Burt Roberts remarked acidly.

The lieutenant ignored the preacher's jibe.

'We have no time to lose. The women upstairs will be wondering what is taking so long here. Yacey! Gravens! Take them all to the wagon, gag and tie them all up … and that includes my woman.'

Lucy Doniphon gave Judd a harsh look of defiance. 'I am not your woman

— not anymore,' she sobbed,

'We will see about that,' Judd replied harshly.

High noon was only a few minutes away when three men with guns prodded the uniformed prisoners across the parade ground of the stockade. Outside the fort, there was silence now as the Paiute warriors waited for Chief Iron Crow's order.

Reverend Burt Roberts was praying out loud. 'Father, I thank you that you have heard me. I know that you always hear me.'

Jed Bliss and Grayson Weathers stumbled. Will Alvord sweated and swore with every step. Dave Calhoun remained silent, not saying one word. The lieutenant ordered Alan Loomis to open the gate, and the wounded soldier went on ahead. Loomis struggled to lift the iron bar with his one good arm.

For a long, terrible moment, the five settlers clad in blue uniforms simply stood and stared at the blood-hungry Paiute Indians. The wind dropped.

Nothing moved.

'So long, fellas!' Judd said, prodding Bliss' back with his rifle.

'C'mon now, walk!' Trooper Ben Copeland told Will Alvord and Dave Calhoun whom he held at gunpoint.

Alan Loomis swallowed. Preacher Roberts had tended his wound. Now he could not look him in the face.

He was ashamed.

It was the reverend who went first. He took a few tentative steps out of the stockade, and then Will Alvord joined him. A hundred Paiute Indians nudged their ponies slowly forward. Judd gave Bliss a shove with his rifle point. The settler fell to his knees and stayed there, crying like a kid. Weathers looked frantically at the oncoming bronze tide and then began to walk.

Calhoun was the last to go. He faced Judd Reed and actually smiled. It was a cold, deadly smile.

'I will see you in hell,' he said and then spat at the officer.

Then he helped Bliss to his feet as

Loomis slammed the gate behind them.

Judd heard another drum beat. It was the slow, ominous advance of a hundred ponies. Suddenly, an earsplitting scream rose above the hoofbeats. Judd watched through a chink in the logs. Uttering hideous cries of triumph, the riders surged towards the five sacrifices. Within seconds, the foremost riders surrounded the white men. They sprang from their horses and swooped on their prey. Four uniformed men were dragged to the ground. Reverend Burt Roberts stayed on his feet, bellowing a prayer and breaking one brave's neck with his bare hands before he went under. The Paiute Indians clawed and punched and bit and kicked in a savage frenzy of hatred. Then Judd saw Iron Claw ride through the milling warriors. The chief spoke an order, and the braves backed away from the five men spread-eagled in the dust. The settlers were all breathing, but their faces were battered and bloody. The blue uniforms were in tatters.

Iron Crow turned in the saddle and

pointed to five small fires. The braves raised their fists in elation and began to drag the victims towards the fires.

'Lieutenant.,' Trooper Alan Loomis stammered, 'those — men out there ... '

'It was us or them,' the lieutenant said bluntly. 'Now, help to load the wagon, Trooper. Get to it!'

As Judd strode across the parade ground, he heard a long, drawn-out scream from outside the stockade walls. Apparently unmoved, he stopped only to pick up a broken shingle lying in the dust. He saw the womenfolk being herded towards the waiting wagon. They had all been gagged, and their wrists were tied behind their backs. Even the children had received the same treatment. When Clara Weathers, red-faced and puffing, sank against the side of the wooden wagon, Trooper Tuck Gravens jabbed her with his rifle.

Anton Kozlov still lay motionless on the floor. Unceremoniously, Judd dragged his rangy body to the trapdoor. The door creaked on rusty hinges as he pulled it open. The hole in the ground stank of musty, stale air. Without hesitating, Judd heaved his former stepfather to the square hole and shoved him down. Anton hit the cellar floor with a dull thud. Judd closed the trapdoor at once. Then he forced the thin edge of the shingle into the gap around the trapdoor, wedging it tight. He returned to the square just as Lucy was being forced into the wagon with the other women.

'Yacey, hold on a minute,' he called, 'I want to say something to my bride.'

'Do you want her to be able to answer you back?' Hal Yacey asked.

Judd Reed nodded. 'Sure, take off her gag.'

Arms folded, Judd waited.

'The gags are just a precaution,' he calmly told Lucy. 'It would not do for a woman to start screaming and yelling just yet. That might let those savages out there know that something is amiss.'

'You pig!' Lucy choked as Yacey ripped away the bandanna.

'Shut your beautiful mouth and listen

to me, Lucy,' Judd said harshly.

'We are headed south to the border. There are bandits and renegades down there who will pay good money for a wagonload of women, and we will know there is nobody left to tell what really happened here.'

His eye raked her as he added, 'On our way back, we will get new uniforms and simply ride up to Fort Bighorn like nothing ever happened. We will say we had to dodge the hostile Paiute Indians and their chief, Iron Crow ... '

He took two steps and stared down at her, face-to-face.

'Lucy, I am gonna give you a choice. It is only for you, not any of the other women, you hear me? You can forget what has happened and ride back as Lieutenant Reed's bride — or you can end up like the rest of the womenfolk, a bandit's whore.'

'Go to hell, Judd Reed!' she cried.

'Don't get all high and mighty with me, Lucy. You think I don't know there has to be a reason for you to come all this way to find a man?' He said that with a certain amount of contempt.

'I will not marry you,' Lucy said with cold dignity. 'The very thought of it makes my skin crawl and my stomach turn!'

'Throw the bitch into the wagon with the other women,' Judd said to Yacey.

The trooper nodded gleefully and said, 'Sure thing, Lieutenant.'

'Think about, this, Miss Doniphon,' Judd said as Hal Yacey gagged her again. 'I will get my money's worth on the way to Mexico. I paid twenty bucks and a hundred bucks delivery fee for you. I will start collecting what is owed me tonight … mark my words.'

Yacey bundled the woman into the wagon without care.

'Reckon we are ready to move out now,' Trooper Tuck Gravens said.

'Loomis, sit inside the wagon and guard the women,' Judd Reed ordered. 'Should not be a big chore and one you can certainly handle. They all have their wrists tied behind their backs and their mouths are gagged.' He addressed Trooper Copeland then: 'You get behind the reins and take it real slow. I just want those horses to pull the wagon nice and easy-like so those savage Indians don't get too curious. Yacey and Gravens, mount up and ride in front of the wagon with me.'

As Gravens leaned from the saddle and opened the gate wide, an agonized scream knifed through the silence. Judd glanced at the Paiute Indian horde. Every bronze warrior had dismounted to ring the five tiny fires. Jed Bliss had already been lifted over his fire and lashed to two stakes. Squirming and screaming, he hung there helplessly as his clothes began to smoke. Death by torture was excruciatingly painful. The slow fires took a long time to roast a man to death.

Judd Reed turned his face away.

Ben Copeland turned the team of horses towards the pass, and the big Conestoga wagon lumbered away from the outpost. Judd heard the muffled groans of the gagged women. Bliss' screams mingled now with the terrified yells of Grayson Weathers.

'They have seen us,' Hal Yacey said.

Several of the Paiute warriors had left the torture fires to gather in a bunch just north of the trail. The sun glittered on their rifles.

'Just ignore them. Keep riding,' the lieutenant advised calmly.

Bellowing like a bull, Reverend Burt Roberts had just been hoisted over his personal hell fire.

'I think they are suspicious.' Tuck Gravens sweated. 'Hell, this isn't natural. Here we are, just riding away while other whites are being tortured to death, lieutenant.'

'We are saving our own hides,' Judd replied tersely. 'Even those savages understand that. Now quit worrying and head for the pass.'

More Indians turned from the fires to watch. Now even Judd felt pin pricks of cold sweat begin to bead his brow. The two mounted warriors urged their ponies into a walk, riding adjacent to the swaying wagon. Suddenly the warriors around the fourth fire raised cries of elation. The Paiute Indians observing the riders and their wagon looked back. All the attention was on Dave Calhoun. He did not scream as the heat seared his cavalry uniform. His apparent disregard of pain held their admiration.

Meanwhile, Judd Reed's riders edged further away, each man with a settler's horse roped behind his own. Within minutes, they had left the grassy flat. The stockade walls receded. The screams of the tortured faded and finally died on the wind. Shadows began to finger Devil's Canyon as the riders approached the mouth of the pass. At the lieutenant's signal, Copeland flicked his reins over the wagon team, urging them to pull harder. They reached the pass, and then Judd pointed to the south. Copeland turned the wagon team.

The shadows then deepened.

'Lieutenant! Lieutenant Reed!'

The hoarse cry came from the lurching wagon. Copeland pulled the team to a halt, and the big Conestoga wagon shuddered to a standstill. Muttering, Judd Reed rode to the rear of the wagon and opened the loose canvas flap.

'What is up, Trooper Loomis?'

Alan Loomis was still rubbing his eyes. He sat hunched over his rifle among the jumble of women who were still bound but no longer gagged.

'Lieutenant,' Loomis confessed. 'I – I fell asleep.'

'Did you stop us to tell me that you had failed to do your duty?' Judd snapped.

'There is a coil of rope on the wagon floor,' Loomis pointed out miserably. 'One of the women must have gotten free and away ... '

Judd climbed into the wagon and scanned the women and children huddled together. He counted them quickly. Then he picked up the curled rope, which was sticky with blood.

'You damn fool!' he raged, smashing a fist into Alan Loomis' upturned face.

8

Canyon of the Dead

Anton Kozlov was in total darkness. He came to, sprawled face down in thick dust. With great difficulty, he had managed to turn over and get his back against the wall. His head throbbed. There was a rather sizeable lump on the back of his neck.

He was in a black hole, and a small hole at that.

The last tiling he remembered was walking into Hal Yacey's gun and seeing the settlers lined up against the wall.

What had happened after that was a mystery to him.

Then he recalled Lucy's frantic warning.

'*Anton!*' Lucy screamed behind him. '*Look out —*'

They must have pitched him into the crudely dug cellar of the stockade. He thumped the trapdoor, tried to force it with his shoulders and then tried to grip the edges of the boards. The wooden door overhead would not budge.

He was trapped.

He traced his fingertips over the boards overhead, probing inch by inch for some hope of escape. One board moved slightly. His senses were still reeling from the blows to the nape of his neck. His mind was fuzzy, and the air seemed fouler all the time. He was drenched with sweat now and getting nowhere. He sat back and told himself that there was plenty of air coming in through the old floorboards. That was not the way he would die.

Suddenly he heard a footfall overhead, and the boards creaked and trembled. Anton called out hoarsely. He did not know who was up there, and did not really care either. He yelled out again at the top of his voice this time. He heard the scrape of wood, and then he could see daylight outlining the trapdoor. Slowly, creakingly, the trapdoor was lifted. Gray light shafted into the hole. Anton saw a bronze face and raven-black hair.

'I am Chante,' the woman told him. 'I belong to Jed Bliss.'

Anton stared at the squaw and rapidly blinked his eyes. 'I am sure glad to see you, ma'am.'

'Please, you come quick,' the squaw pleaded. 'You save my man, please!'

Anton Kozlov hauled himself out of the stockade's cellar. Plastered with dust, he sat for a moment inhaling pure air. Not losing a moment, Chante told him what had happened with the five male settlers and the troopers.

She concluded, ' ... the lieutenant and the other soldiers rode out of here pretending to be settlers. They took all women in a wagon. The lieutenant say we would be sold in Mexico.' She smiled. 'Soldiers do not tie good knots. Chante slip free when wounded guard fall asleep. Please hurry! My man burns!'

Anton stood up. Slapping the cellar dust from his buckskins, he strode outside. The chill evening wind carried the screams of tortured men.

'No good for me to talk to Iron Crow,' she explained. 'That is why Chante come straight to cellar. You are a warrior, an old warrior, but still a warrior,' she said. 'Iron Crow will listen to you.'

'I will do what I can, but make no promises,' Anton said.

He loped across the parade ground in the fading light. The gates were just as Judd had left them, wide open. Motioning Chante to stay in the stockade, Anton walked outside. Beds of hot coals lit the five bodies from below. Three of the suspended men were writhing. One hung limply. The last man held his body taut and motionless. Smoke curled languidly around them all. Cold, terrible fury gripped Anton as he paced across the flat. According to Bliss' squaw, Judd had condemned these innocent men to death by torture for the vile crime he and his blue-coats had committed. Not content with this evil, he also planned to assign decent, respectable women to a life of miserable debauchery.

Judd Reed was a man without a conscience. They shared a love for the same woman, one as a son and the other as a husband, but the similarity ended right there. Right now, he hated Judd Reed enough to kill his former stepson.

As he approached the Fires, most of the warriors were lounging on the grass, content to eat, talk and watch the five men dying.

Iron Crow had called off the hostilities, but that did not make Anton Kozlov a welcome guest. As soon as they saw him, several braves leapt to their feet to surround him. Anton kept walking, shouldering his way through the growing crowd.

Ignoring the brandished weapons, Anton made straight for Iron Crow. The chief sat among the elders, in the flickering glow of the first torture fire. As he stepped into the firelight, Anton glimpsed the squirming body of Chante's man, Jed Bliss. The front of his uniform hung in charred, smoking tatters from the raw, red flesh of his chest and belly.

'Kozlov — help me — ' Bliss begged.

As Anton walked around the fire, Iron Crow looked up without expression. Beside him sat Plenty Arrows, the brave who was to marry his granddaughter.

'I come in peace, Chief Iron Crow,' Anton said.

'Why do you come at all?' Iron Crow demanded. 'Did you not run away with the rest of the white-eye settlers?'

'Chief Iron Crow, the men who rode away were not settlers. They were the soldiers you sought,' Anton explained.

The old chieftain stared at him with unblinking eyes.

'What is the paleface saying?' Wind Shawl wheezed.

'We were tricked, and so were you,' Anton said bluntly. 'The guilty soldiers held us at gunpoint. I was thrown into a cellar. The settlers were forced to put on the soldiers' uniforms to fool you.' He looked around at the incredulous tribal elders. 'You are torturin' innocent men. The real soldiers rode out with that wagon. The settlers' women are in that wagon too, and the soldiers mean to sell them in Mexico.'

Iron Crow climbed to his feet. He looked at the writhing body of Jed Bliss and then at the four others. He nodded slowly.

'This paleface speaks with a forked tongue!' Wind Shawl accused venomously, pointing a shaking finger at Anton.

'Ask Chante. She is a Crow who escaped from the wagon,' Anton Kozlov challenged. 'She waits at the stockade gates.'

'My blood brother, Looks at the Bear, said you are a good man,' Iron Crow asserted. 'That is enough.' He turned to the enraged shaman and said, 'Iron Crow bids you to be silent!' He addressed the circle of braves. 'Cut down the paleface prisoners.'

Wind Shawl screeched his fury, but the warriors hurried to obey.

'The prisoners are all alive,' Yellow Hawk told Anton. 'They would not have died until the fifth day.'

'Kozlov, we will pursue the real murderers,' Iron Crow vowed as his braves brandished weapons again. 'We will hunt them down and bring them back to burn on our fires.'

'Let me speak, Iron Crow,' Anton requested as Bliss was carried from his fire.

The Paiute Indian chieftain nodded his head slowly. 'Iron Crow listens.'

'The killers are headed for Mexico,' Anton said. 'By now, they know of Chante's escape. They will play it safe and go quickly towards Mexico, through the long valley you call the Canyon of the Dead.'

Sudden stillness gripped the camp.

'The sacred place!' Yellow Hawk whispered.

'The spirits of the dead still live there,' Wind Shawl muttered.

'Bad medicine!' another withered Paiute elder added in a hushed voice.

'My braves will not ride into the Canyon of the Dead,' Iron Crow said firmly.

'But we can wait where the canyon ends,' a Paiute Indian called Sky Raven suggested. Anton had heard of this man from past dealings in the area.

'Hear me,' Anton said. 'Those men raped and murdered your maidens. In that way, they dishonored you. Now they have caused innocent settlers to be tortured and have stolen the valley women.' He raised his right fist. 'Now they have dishonored white men also.'

Iron Crow nodded sagely. 'This is so.'

'The Canyon of the Dead is not for you, but I will ride there with any white settlers who can ride with me,' offered Anton.

'There will be two such men,' The Paiute leader predicted. 'The silent paleface and the one who bellows like an angry bull.'

'Chief Iron Crow, the time for torture is over,' Anton Kozlov told him. 'You want justice. The white settlers want justice. Let that justice be swift and sure.'

The chieftain contemplated Anton's pronouncement.

Finally, he said, 'It shall be so, Anton Kozlov.'

Anton went from fire to fire. The last of the roasted settlers, Will Alvord, had just been cut down. He swore and tried to stand, only to collapse in pain. Jed Bliss lay weeping in the grass. Grayson Weathers was badly burned and simply lay where the Paiute Indians had placed him. Dave Calhoun reared up as Anton approached. Reverend Burt Roberts was the last on his feet.

'I am goin' after those lousy side-winders before they sell the women in Mexico,' Anton addressed the settlers. 'I am lookin' for anyone willin' to join me.'

At first, all he heard were Bliss' sobs of pain.

'Count me in, Anton,' Reverend Roberts volunteered. 'It is the Lord's work!'

'I will ride with you,' Calhoun said simply.

Anton turned to the Paiute Indian chief. 'You were right, Iron Crow. Two are ready to ride. However, they will need clothes and we will all need horses and guns.'

'Yellow Hawk will see that you have

all you need,' Iron Crow delegated.

Only minutes passed before Anton Kozlov was astride a pinto pony. Like Calhoun and Roberts, he was also given a rifle and ammunition.

'Thank you, Chief Iron Crow,' Anton said, making ready to ride.

'Yellow Hawk and a war party will ride for four days and nights to wait south of the sacred place,' Iron Crow said. 'If you fail, they will stop the bad men there.'

'We will not fail, Iron Crow,' Anton proclaimed.

'We will care for these men you leave behind,' the elder Paiute called Sky Raven promised. 'They will be walking when you return.'

They rode out under the rising moon. Preacher Burt Roberts grunted in pain whenever they crossed rough ground. Dave Calhoun winced but no sound escaped his thin, bloodless lips. Leaving the camp behind, they cut across the flat to follow the wagon tracks.

Anton drew rein briefly by the stockade gates and called, 'Chante, go to your man. He needs you. Don't be afraid, Iron Crow's warriors will not harm you.'

On the edge of the Paiute Indian camp, Plenty Arrows watched them ride out. The eyes of the man who had been betrothed to a princess were inscrutably dark.

9

Clash in the Canyon

The forlorn soldier, that so
   nobly fought,
He would have well becom'd this
   place, and graced
The thankings of a king ...
                              Cymbeline

Coming out of the pine-dotted pass,
Anton Kozlov led the riders into a long,
deep-walled valley. This was a wild place,
and it offered no welcome to living men.
The crater-like canyon was believed to
have been formed from the collapse of
the Mount Mazama volcano. One legend
that Anton had heard many years before
from the Klamath Tribe, witnessed the
eruption due to a great battle between
Chief Llao — of the Below world —
and Chief Skell — of the Above world,
where the battle ended with the destruc-

tion of Mount Mazama. Another legend claims the water came from the tears of wolves. It was the catapulted volcanic ash miles into the sky that expelled so much pumice and ash that the summit soon collapsed, created a huge smoldering caldera.

Eventually, rain and snowmelt accumulated in the caldera, forming a lake. Wildflowers, along with hemlock, fir, and pine, recolonized surroundings. Black bears and bobcats, deer and marmots, eagles and hawks returned to the canyon.

Heading out of a thicket, Anton saw the first skeleton. The chalk-white bones were resting on a frame of interwoven branches. Hollowed eyes stared at the three white men as they rode past. Probing deeper into the valley, they saw coyotes slinking away from rotting flesh. They circled the bones of six Indians.

Suddenly a scream echoed out over the valley.

'Dear God!' the preacher whispered, drawing rein. His face was ashen.

'What–what was that?'

'It did not come from no dead Injun,' Dave Calhoun assured him.

'It is a woman,' Anton said. 'I would say Clara Weathers is giving birth.'

They followed the wagon tracks. Another high-pitched scream tore the night apart as the three riders splashed across a creek and headed due south beside the fresh wheel ruts. Another coyote slunk across their path.

Anton Kozlov glimpsed the hooped canvas of the Conestoga wagon and halted his pinto pony. Lifting his rifle, Calhoun drew rein and waited for Reverend Burt Roberts.

'They are just down there,' Anton indicated. 'We will leave the horses here. Reverend, you move straight in and get yourself set up behind that boulder over yonder. Calhoun, we will circle the camp.'

They dropped from the backs of their ponies, and Calhoun and Anton headed into the tall, spiky grass. Soon they could make out four men seated around a very small fire. One man sat apart from the rest, smoking a cigar. The wagon creaked, and Clara cried out in pain. Anton and Calhoun began to drift around to the opposite side of the camp. They reached a towering pine.

'This is your spot,' Anton indicated to Calhoun softly.

'Fine,' Calhoun agreed without hesitation.

'We will need to be careful, so no stray lead goes into that wagon full of women, understood?' Anton said.

'Kozlov,' Dave Calhoun murmured, 'killin' used to be my business. None of my bullets will stray off target, I promise you that.'

Anton saw the harsh truth in the settler's eyes. He crawled through the grass to a rocky slab overlooking the camp. Snatches of conversation drifted up to him.

'Hell!' Trooper Hal Yacey croaked. 'Would somebody shut that damn woman up?'

'She won't be loud much longer,'

211

Tuck Gravens said. 'Anyway, she will sell better when the kid's born and she is back to normal size.'

'Please … please let me go.' It was Lucy Doniphon's voice now.

Looking down his rifle, Anton spotted her, bound hand and foot in the shadows of the wagon.

Judd Reed took a swig from his whiskey bottle.

'Forget about that squawking bitch,' he said. 'I figure it is time for you and me to start getting acquainted.'

'No!' she cried, her body shrinking into the grass.

Judd grabbed her hair and pulled her ruthlessly to her feet. He set the bottle down carefully and grabbed at her bodice. The two top buttons popped and flew into the tall grass.

Anton wormed across the flat ledge as Lucy's blouse fell away from the lush curves of her full breasts. Judd's eyes glittered with lust. Anton reached the edge of the rock balcony, and a split moment later, Calhoun stepped out from behind the pine.

It was Hal Yacey who howled a frantic warning. 'Lieutenant!'

Anton Kozlov's rifle boomed and Trooper Hal Yacey was silenced for good. The trooper crashed forward into the cooking fire, smothering the flames like a wet sack. Gravens and Ben Copeland were on their feet already, but Reverend Burt Roberts triggered. Gravens caught the preacher's slug high in the shoulder. Tottering like a crazy drunk, he tried to level his .45. Cool as death, Dave Calhoun took aim and killed the trooper with one shot.

Copeland had his back against a wagon wheel. He held one rifle to his shoulder, and had another in reserve. Bullets raked the clearing and skipped from the rock ledge just inches from Anton's face. The frontiersman raised himself on his knees and took deliberate aim. His two bullets tore into Copeland's heart. Only two soldiers remained now. Judd had not fired a shot. Instead, he grabbed Lucy and held her struggling body in front of him.

'Loomis! Shoot, damn you trooper!' he bellowed.

'No, Lieutenant, I won't … ' Alan Loomis decided, tossing away his gun, knowing he could not throw away his guilt.

'You yellow little snake!' Judd Reed screamed in fury.

He had one arm clamped across Lucy's throat holding her like a vice. His free hand held a Colt .45.

'Die, you coward!' He raged and turned his gun on Alan Loomis.

The young trooper lurched forward with blood welling from his mouth.

Judd backed away from the fire, dragging his squirming human shield with him.

'I am getting out of here, and I am taking this woman with me,' he snarled. 'Don't try to shoot, and that goes for you, too, Reverend, unless you want to kill this woman … '

There was a dull, sickly thud. Judd's six-gun fell from his outstretched fingers and dropped to the grass. Glassy-eyed, the lieutenant began to sway from side to side. Lucy Doniphon stepped away from the cavalry officer. Without her support, Judd Reed pitched headlong with an arrow embedded deeply between his shoulder blades.

'Plenty Arrows is not afraid of the spirits of the dead,' the young brave said. 'The woman I love now dwells among the dead.'

He slid his second arrow back into the buckskin quiver and nodded disdainfully at Judd's spread-eagled body 'Once a man like this is dead, his evil dies with him.' The white men watched him in incredulous silence.

'Go in peace, Plenty Arrows,' Anton said finally. 'You ride with much honor.' The warrior nodded and went on his way.

Just then, Henrietta Roberts emerged from the Conestoga wagon. She alone had been allowed to act as midwife to Clara Weathers. Now she held up two wet, slippery babies.

'The Lord be praised!' she announced. 'Twins — a boy and a girl and all healthy!'

The preacher strode towards her, yelling the good news that all the men were safe. Anton saw Plenty Arrows vanish like a specter — fittingly enough in the Canyon of the Dead — and then Lucy was in his arms. He kissed her — his mind raced to his long-dead wife, Lesya and he hoped she would approve — and held Lucy, feeling her heart beating against his chest.

'I meant what I said, Anton Kozlov! I wished you were the man I had come out here to marry!'

He kissed her willing mouth again as the others made ready to leave. His thoughts of his late wife remained in his thoughts and he could feel she would be OK with him finding love again.

'Reverend Roberts will have a new home to raise, same as all of us,' Calhoun said. 'But I am sure he will find time for a wedding.'

'I don't know about that,' Anton said, trying to be humorous.

'The age difference does not bother me, Anton,' Lucy whispered to him, sensing his apprehension.

The mountain man wrapped his buckskin coat tenderly around her bare shoulders, and then he spotted Socks — his sorrel — tethered to the wagon. Next to Lucy, his horse was his most treasured friend. Lucy followed him as he went towards the horse who greeted them with a whinny. They both patted the horse's head and stroked its mane.

Somehow, Anton knew they were going to be riding double, back to Devil's Canyon and his tiny cabin — and that thought did not bother him at all.

But first, Anton knew they would have to make one stop before returning to his cabin.

10

Fort Bighorn

The garrison of Fort Bighorn had time to recognize its weariness. The men on watch along the catwalks yawned and fidgeted. Those in reserve wrapped themselves in blankets and lay close around their fires to sleep. But their slumbers were not restful. Again and again, they started to wake to ask what was happening as they had all seen the fires burning and smoke rising from the old stockade.

They wondered about the potential casualties and that daunted Major Amos Peabody. Most thought a Paiute attack on the fort was imminent. The major dared not risk sending out any more troopers in the worsening weather after his dispatch of four troopers had not returned. He felt it more prudent to keep them at the fort. He had already dispatched troopers to forts to the south, east, and west, and had held off charges from both Crow and Paiute in recent months, and this meant a diminished accuracy of defense fire. Now Peabody had less than a hundred and twenty to man the walls of his fort.

'I wish the army would send more troops before the Indians or the weather kills us all off,' mourned Peabody. 'We might be able to hit one or two of them Indians if they move on from the stockade and turn their attention towards us.'

Peabody turned his field glasses upon a group of mounted riders approaching the fort.

'Who are they, Major?' a trooper close to Peabody asked through chattering teeth.

'They are not Indians,' the major noted and all sighed upon the catwalk.

'Shall we let them in?' another trooper asked.

The major nodded and the order was relayed to the gate.

Anton Kozlov, riding double with Lucy Doniphon, along with Dave Calhoun, rode slowly inside Fort Bighorn. The Reverend Burt Roberts and the other women and the newborn twins had continued to the valley.

'We bring news of your troopers,' Anton said as he helped Lucy off the sorrel before dismounting himself. They were greeted by Major Peabody and several troopers, although all eyes were upon the visitors.

The major nodded and motioned the group inside. Once there, they were treated to hot coffee and some rolls to eat. The major allowed his visitors to drink and eat before he continued with the news.

'Now,' he supplied, 'you mentioned that you have news of my troopers. What news do you have?'

'I am sorry to say that your troopers ... ' Anton began, then paused.

'It is OK, come right out and say it,' the major demanded. 'They are dead, I presume.'

Anton nodded. 'They were killed by the Paiute.' He shot a quick look to the major. 'But it was warranted. Those troopers raped and murdered several Paiute maidens. Their murders were justified.'

The major stood up. 'That is not for you to decide, sir!' He straightened his uniform. 'How do we know that what you report is true?'

'Why would we come here and tell you if it weren't?' Anton fired back.

'It is the truth,' Lucy added, holding her cup of coffee to warm her frigid hands.

The major grunted. 'Still, did you see this for yourselves? And if so, how come the Paiute allowed you all to live?'

'The Paiute aren't evil, Major,' Anton said. 'Lieutenant Judd Reed and his men were not good men. They did awful things to the Paiute women and tried to do so to Lucy and the other women of Devil's Canyon.'

'Then it is a sad day for the US Cavalry,' the major noted. 'Once the weather clears, we will go and mark the graves of these troopers. I just hope their actions will not affect our relationship with the Paiute people. Chief Iron Crow is a good man, but a hard man nonetheless.'

'Aye,' Anton said. 'That he is.'

'You must be tired and cold,' Major Peabody replied. 'Please enjoy our hospitality for a while. It has been ages since we have had visitors here.'

'We could use some medical treatment,' Dave Calhoun muttered.

'Of course, we have a fine sawbones here,' the major said, turning to one of the troopers who stood by the door. 'Sergeant, go and fetch Reeves.' The trooper saluted and left to follow his order.

Later they gathered in the fort's hospital, where not just the visitors had received treatment, other wounded men, moaned, grumbled, or simulated cheerfulness. Lucy Doniphon sat next to one severely injured trooper. Anton and Major Peabody heard her singing softly:

And there I will tell you a tale
Must be told by the moonlight
    alone,

'In the grove at the end of the vale....'

Between her hands she held the trooper's slack, dough-pale fist. His eyes above the masking bandages watched her tenderly, she then turned to look at Anton.

'It was my little sister's favorite song,' she whispered.

'Beautiful,' he smiled. 'Trooper, you are on your way up again. Hang in there, son.'

The major nodded his agreement and gently patted the young soldier on his leg.

'They fell like wheat the last time out against the Paiute,' Peabody told Kozlov. 'We will make out. Keep on getting well.' And to Lucy, 'You are just what he needs. Finish that song, he seems to like it too.'

★   ★   ★

The next morning, after breakfast was over, Anton Kozlov pulled out a cigar the major had given him, felt for a match. Then he returned the cigar to his inside

223

pocket. He would wait until this damned cold was gone, and he could sit on the porch of his tiny cabin, after rebuilding it, of course, and relish that cigar.

Only a handful of troopers were manning the walls now, as Major Peabody was no longer concerned with an imminent attack. He was still vigilant, but his fears had subsided a little. He was in charge; he had already given the cook a growl about his bacon.

The rest of the command was pulled back to the parade ground, for a reserve to go where it would be needed most. Anton was catching a cold, Lucy heard his sneezing; he mopped his ninny nose with a handkerchief. Goddamn cold.

The sun was coming up, and it was time to go home.

The major had offered a detachment to travel with the three and they accepted as they did not wish to be rude. Anton assured Peabody that he would speak with Iron Crow and try to convince him that four bad troopers did not mean all the US cavalrymen were just alike.

After exchanging handshakes with the major and mounting their horses, the three — Anton, Lucy and Calhoun — joined by four troopers, all rode through the gates of Fort Bighorn, starting their trek back to the valley where they would live, hopefully, peacefully for many years to come.

We do hope that you have enjoyed reading this large print book.

Did you know that all of our titles are available for purchase?

We publish a wide range of high quality large print books including:
Romances, Mysteries, Classics
General Fiction
Non Fiction and Westerns

Special interest titles available in large print are:
The Little Oxford Dictionary
Music Book, Song Book
Hymn Book, Service Book

Also available from us courtesy of Oxford University Press:
Young Readers' Dictionary
(large print edition)
Young Readers' Thesaurus
(large print edition)

For further information or a free brochure, please contact us at:
Ulverscroft Large Print Books Ltd.,
The Green, Bradgate Road, Anstey,
Leicester, LE7 7FU, England.
Tel: (00 44) **0116 236 4325**
Fax: (00 44) **0116 234 0205**